W9-BST-856

CGSD LIBRARY

Life Goes On

Life Goes On

A HARMONY NOVEL

Philip Gulley

HarperSanFrancisco
A Division of HarperCollins*Publishers*

HarperCollins Web site: http://www.harpercollins.com
HarperCollins®, ✒®, and HarperSanFrancisco™ are
trademarks of HarperCollins Publishers, Inc.

FIRST EDITION

Book design by Susan Rimerman

Library of Congress Cataloging-in-Publication Data
Gulley, Philip.
Life Goes On / by Philip Gulley
p. cm.
ISBN 0–06–000635–8 (cloth)
1. Harmony (Ind.: Imaginary place)—Fiction. 2. City and town life—Fiction.
3. Quakers—Fiction. 4. Clergy—Fiction. 5. Indiana—Fiction. I. Title
PS3557.U449 L54 2004
813'.54—dc22   2003064896

04 05 06 07 08 RRD(H) 10 9 8 7 6 5 4 3 2 1

For Joan and the boys

CONTENTS

Life Goes On

One

Easter

$\mathcal{M}$y earliest memory of Easter was when I was five years old and looking for Easter eggs in my grandparents' backyard. I'm not sure if what I'm remembering is the event itself or the photograph of it my father took — my brother, Roger, and me, dressed in our Sunday suits, pausing just long enough from our egg gathering to record the moment for posterity.

My grandmother kept the picture on the top of her bureau, a black-and-white photo with scalloped edges. In the background was my grandfather's shed, where he had a cot for naps on summer afternoons amidst the pleasant aroma of gasoline, turpentine, and sawdust.

I would visit them on Saturday afternoons and sit in the backyard swing with my grandma while Grandpa push-mowed the yard in neat stripes, the blades snicking against the roller. Every now and then he'd happen upon a long-forgotten Easter egg. A rainbow of egg shell would arc up from the mower while a pungent, sulfuric odor filled the air, the delayed resurrection of a half-buried Easter egg.

Alice Stout was my Sunday school teacher when I was growing up at Harmony Friends Meeting. When she would ask me why we celebrated Easter, I knew I was supposed to say something about Jesus rising from the tomb. But that struck me as a fanciful yarn the adults concocted to liven up the religion. For me, Easter was about sitting at the kitchen table with my mother and brother the night before, dipping eggs in teacups of dye, then laying them out to dry on that week's copy of the *Harmony Herald*.

Now Alice Stout is in the nursing home at Cartersburg, four eggs short of a dozen. When I went to visit her the week before Easter and read to her from the Scriptures about the Resurrection, she cackled like a madwoman. "Bullfeathers," she said. It is troublesome to struggle all your life believing something, only to have your Sunday school teacher dismiss it as bullfeathers, even if she is out of her gourd.

One of the ironies of life is that we often return gladly to what we once fled. I returned to my hometown and became the pastor of my childhood church. Now it's my job to rally the troops and urge them to believe things they might otherwise doubt, at least according to Dale Hinshaw, our self-appointed guardian of doctrinal purity, who's been vigilant about keeping me orthodox, lest I stray into the wilds of rationalism.

On my fourth Easter as pastor, I suggested we hold special services during Holy Week. I'm not sure now what possessed me to do that, probably my naive habit of thinking the church is always one program away from vitality. I envisioned a little Scripture reading, some singing, then a spirited theological discussion on certain aspects of the Resurrection.

When I presented my idea to the elders, they waded in with their concerns. Asa Peacock wanted to know if we could have cookies. Dale Hinshaw made me promise we'd read from the King James Version of the Bible. Harvey Muldock suggested holding a raffle each night to draw more people, and Fern Hampton declared, rather emphatically, that if the kitchen were used, the Friendly Women's Circle was not going to be stuck cleaning it.

Even though I grew up in this church and am accustomed to its eccentricities, I continue to marvel at how the simplest idea can soon rival the complexity of a Middle East peace treaty. What began as a modest suggestion to read the Bible, pray, and reflect on the meaning of Easter soon involved three committees, a church-wide vote on cookie preference, and an agreement to collect a special offering for the Friendly Women's Circle Cabinet Fund.

Fern Hampton was placed in charge of the cookie vote. Miriam Hodge suggested she might not want to make a big deal about it, just take an informal poll among the ladies of the church.

"What about the men?" Harvey Muldock asked. "How come we don't get any say?"

"I'm sorry, Harvey," Miriam said. "I didn't mean to exclude you. What kind of cookies would you like?"

"I thought it was my job to ask people what kind of cookies they wanted," Fern complained.

"By all means," Miriam said. "I just thought I'd help."

Fern turned to Harvey. "What kind of cookies would you like, Harvey?"

Harvey thought for a moment. "How about those little chocolate cookies with oatmeal that you mix up and put in the refrigerator?"

"One vote for chocolate drop cookies," Fern said, rooting through her purse for paper and a pencil. "Dale, what kind of cookies would you like?"

"Fern, perhaps we could do this a bit later," Miriam suggested. "I'm sure Sam has more pressing business for us to discuss just now."

"Don't I get to say what kind of cookies I like?" Dale asked.

"You go right ahead, Dale," Fern said. "I'm sure Sam won't mind."

"Well, I was over in Cartersburg last week at the Bible bookstore and they had these Scripture cookies. Kind of like fortune cookies, except they got the Word in 'em instead. I think we oughta get us some of them."

I used to believe the world would be saved by church committees, though sixteen years of ministry have cured me of such optimism. Now I prize those rare and selfless saints, those unwavering levers, who move the world while the committees are deciding on carpet colors.

After Fern's cookie survey, we moved on to the pressing matter of the special collection for the kitchen cabinets.

"Sam, what are your thoughts on the ushering?" Dale asked. "You want a box at the back of the meetinghouse for folks to put their donations in, or were you wantin' the guys to pass the baskets?"

"Well, if you ask me," Fern interrupted, "I think we should pass the baskets. That way people can't sneak out the side door without giving."

The elders sat quietly, pondering this vital concern.

"How about a box at the back," I said. "It feels less pushy."

"Sam, if it was up to you, we wouldn't ever get new kitchen cabinets," Fern grumbled. "Why can't you get behind the mission of the church a little more?"

And so the rest of the evening went. Miriam Hodge struggled valiantly to sail our church through choppy waters, while Dale and Fern seemed bent on running us aground.

Despite my misgivings, the Monday night service went off without a hitch. Harvey Muldock read the Scripture, pronouncing the names like a New Testament scholar. Dale had placed a small, tasteful box at the back of the meeting room for donations and didn't even stand to point it out. Bea Majors refrained from playing the organ during the quiet time. And Fern Hampton's favorite show was on television, so she stayed home.

Tuesday morning Dale stopped by my office to tell me we had collected forty-three cents and a button. "Hester Gladden put the button in there," he informed me. "She's always doing that."

I pointed out that it was only the first night and not to worry.

"I thought I'd maybe stand and make an announcement tonight," he said. "Maybe just show folks where the box is."

"Gee, Dale, I don't know. Why don't you and I just pray about it and trust the Lord to take care of things."

Personally, I didn't think the Lord gave a hoot whether we raised enough money for new kitchen cabinets, but it beat Dale putting the squeeze on people during a worship service.

So we prayed, Dale and I, that people would be open to God's leading and not leave by the side door, but would instead walk past the collection box and drop in nothing smaller than a twenty.

Tuesday night's service was a joy to behold. Miriam Hodge led a lively discussion; then her daughter Amanda played the flute. No one coughed or blew his nose while the Scripture was being read. And Fern Hampton stayed down in the kitchen the whole time, making punch to go with the cookies.

The next morning my office phone rang. It was Dale.

"We've got problems, Sam. Big problems."

"What's wrong?"

"You know that forty-three cents we collected Monday night?"

"Yeah."

"Well, I left it in the box to kinda give people a hint, and somebody took it. We're down to one button."

"Let's not despair, Dale. This might be the Lord testing us."

Wednesday night, a crack in the dam appeared. Bea Majors left her sheet music at home, so she played the only song she knew from memory—"Surrey with the Fringe on Top" from *Oklahoma!* Asa Peacock lost his place in the Scripture reading and began reading from the Song of Solomon. And Fern stood and complained that someone had dropped a cookie on the kitchen floor the night before and hadn't bothered to pick it up. "We don't have a maid service here, folks. You gotta clean up your messes."

Dale came by on Thursday morning to tell me Hester Gladden had asked for her button back.

That night, in the tradition of our Quaker ancestors, we had silent worship for an hour. Not many people came, and those who did spent the hour glancing at their watches. I put a twenty-dollar

bill in the collection box to buoy up Dale's spirits.

The evening of Good Friday, the meetinghouse was full. Dale nailed me as soon as I came through the door. "We got a big crowd here, Sam. Why not let's take up an offering?"

Fern was right behind him. "I say we don't let 'em leave until they've coughed up enough money for the cabinets."

Harvey Muldock lumbered over, grasped my arm, and pulled me close. "Bea Majors just called," he whispered. "She's sick. But don't worry, Asa's gone home to get his harmonica."

Perhaps the day will come when I no longer repress the memory of that dreadful evening, an evening in which the crucifixion of Jesus seemed a comparative highlight.

Saturday morning I woke up with a scratchy throat and a cough, having spent the week shaking hands with people at the back of the meetinghouse, some of whom had just sneezed into their hands. By mid-afternoon, I was losing my voice and arose on Easter morning unable to speak above a whisper.

Barbara, my wife, phoned the elders, told them of my plight, and asked them to meet me at the meetinghouse as soon as possible. When I arrived, the elders were clustered in my office. I mouthed a "hello."

Fern Hampton was the first to speak. "Sam Gardner, this is the most inconsiderate thing you've ever done. Losing your voice on Easter Sunday. What were you thinking?"

Dale brightened. "One time on the Reverend Rod Duvall's television ministry he cast demons out of a deaf-mute and had him talkin' in a minute flat. Maybe Sam's got demons."

"It wouldn't surprise me in the least," Fern said.

Before I could object, Dale raised his right hand, placed it on my head, and began praying. "Lord, we just ask You to cast this demon out of Sam that's trying to keep him from preaching your Word. We just ask You to nip Satan's follies in the bud." He slid his hand down the back of my head, squeezed my neck, and commanded various foul spirits to depart from me.

"Say something, Sam," Fern demanded.

"It's no good," I whispered.

"Chop him one in the throat," she advised Dale. "That'll send those rascals packin'."

"Why don't we just have silent worship?" Miriam Hodge asked.

Harvey Muldock paled at the prospect of having to sit quietly for an hour. "How about you preaching, Dale?" he asked.

Miriam Hodge spoke quickly, before Dale could respond. "Let's not ask Dale to do that, Harvey. It wouldn't be kind. He hasn't had any time to prepare."

"Can you do it, Dale?" Fern asked.

Dale squared his shoulders. "Don't ever let it be said that Dale Hinshaw wasn't ready, willing, and able to preach the Word. I'll do it."

And that was how Dale Hinshaw came to preach on the biggest Sunday of the year.

It could have been worse. Poisonous snakes numbering in the thousands could have slithered from the heat ducts and crawled up our legs. Tarantulas could have dropped from the ceiling onto our heads. We could have been dipped in honey and staked out over a hill of African fire ants. It was bad, but it could have been worse.

He began with the Crucifixion, a topic I thought we had covered sufficiently on Good Friday. I kept hoping he would mention the Resurrection, a not unreasonable expectation on Easter Sunday. Unfortunately, he had the scent of blood in his nostrils and couldn't be diverted. He began to weep, thanking God for having His son killed so we could come to church and have committee meetings and raise money for new kitchen cabinets.

He spoke for forty-five minutes. He would have gone on longer, but Bea Majors has played the offertory every Sunday morning at precisely eleven-twenty for forty-one years, and she wasn't about to let a little thing like an unfinished sermon keep her from her sacred duty.

Dale launched into a closing prayer, thanking the Lord for letting us live in a free nation, where we were free to worship as we pleased and believe what we wanted, provided, of course, that what we believed could be supported by the King James Bible. Then he invited the congregation to join him in the Pledge of Allegiance. Then, mercifully, it was over.

I took the next day off to clean the basement. My mother came over to help. When my grandmother had died, we'd stored the leftovers of her life in boxes, spending a day every now and then sorting through them. In the second box we looked in we found the picture of Roger and me, dressed in our Sunday suits, standing in front of my grandfather's shed, Easter baskets clutched in our hands.

We had two stacks going—the "keep" stack and the "Goodwill" stack. I put the picture in the "keep" stack. As we worked our way through the boxes, keeping and giving away, I thought about how much of life involved holding on and letting go. The trick is in knowing what goes where. Sometimes we cling to what should be surrendered and shed what ought to be kept.

"How about this?" my mother asked, breaking the spell of my thought. She held up a bowling trophy my grandmother had won in 1956.

"Probably time to let it go," I said.

"You sure you don't want it?"

"Not me. How about you?"

"I don't know what I'd do with it," she admitted.

"Then it's probably time to let it go."

"How about we give it to Roger?" she asked.

"Good thinking."

So we started a third stack—one for the things we once treasured, but now, finding them no longer useful, are content to let go.

Two

The Sunday School Queen

The week after Easter was quiet. The church members, recuperating from the frenzy of Holy Week, were lying low since a rumor was circulating that we might need a new Sunday school teacher to replace Alice Stout. People had been avoiding me all week, not wanting to get roped into the job.

Judy Iverson is the head of the Christian Education Committee and has been trying to ease Alice Stout out of the picture. Dale Hinshaw picks her up at the nursing home and brings her to church, where she continues to teach Sunday school out of pure habit. Parents are not enthusiastic about their children being left in the care of a woman who begins each class by asking the children to pray for our president, Franklin Delano Roosevelt, and for our country as we defend ourselves against the dreaded Huns. She also dwells a bit long on the stories of God smiting people.

Judy Iverson suggested to Dale he might pick up Alice an hour later.

"Then we'd both miss Sunday school," he'd said, which would have solved two problems nicely.

It has never been easy to find Sunday school teachers, because, in the history of our church, no one has ever been allowed to stop teaching unless they moved or died. Mental defects are not a sufficient reason, the assumption being that one was likely deranged to have agreed to teach in the first place.

Judy Iverson and her husband, Paul, have twins, who are now three years old and housebroken, which has freed Judy to volunteer at the church. The position of chair of the Christian Education Committee had been vacant since 1994, when Harold Morrison died. Every time a replacement was suggested, Asa Peacock decried the church's haste in replacing Harold while he was still warm in the grave.

We had to wait until Asa was on vacation, which was a long wait, since Asa and Jessie aren't the vacationing types. But the last week of April, with the planting done, he and Jessie drove west to see Mount Rushmore, which they had been planning to do for years. With Asa out of state, the Nominating Committee named Judy Iverson to head up the Christian Education Committee, and in she went.

Her first order of business was to order a new curriculum, which caused a stir among the teachers, who had used the current material for twenty years and could teach it in their sleep. Judy didn't even order the new curriculum from the Bible bookstore in Cartersburg. She imported it from the Unitarians in Boston. It had lessons on caring for the earth and learning to live as one with all the human family and respecting diversity and seeing God's presence in rocks and trees.

I knew there would be trouble the moment I saw it.

I thumbed through it at my desk, while Judy sat across from me.

"Very nice," I said. "It appears to be well written, thoughtful, and progressive. I'm sure the children will enjoy it. But aren't you concerned that it doesn't mention Jesus?"

"Not at all," she said. "Should I be?"

Judy grew up in California and met her husband at college while earning a degree in peace studies, which enabled her to find employment in the fast-food industry.

They had moved to Harmony to escape the city and live closer to nature. Her husband, Paul, was the sixth-grade teacher. Judy tried raising goats and spinning their wool to knit sweaters. The goats died, so she tried selling herbs. When that went bust, she decided to volunteer. She serves on the Library Board with Miss Rudy, works at the church, and hauls the twins to the Montessori school in Cartersburg three days a week.

The April meeting of the Christian Education Committee was held on a Tuesday morning in the meetinghouse basement. I arrived early to make coffee, hoping it would distract people from the new curriculum.

Judy asked if she could begin our meeting with a guided meditation. She asked us to close our eyes and envision a mountain meadow. "Feel the peace running through your body. It's starting at your fingertips and working it's way into your inner being."

I heard Frank, my secretary, snicker.

"Yes, that's good," Judy said. "Don't contain your joy. Now gather all your destructive ideas about God and release them to the wind."

I opened my eyes slightly and peeked across the table at Dolores

Hinshaw, who sat with her arms folded across her chest, glowering, clearly not happy at the prospect of releasing all her destructive ideas about God, lest she not have any ideas left.

I heard a sound, like wind blowing through trees. Judy's lips were pursed, and she was blowing outward. "Can you feel them leaving your body?" she asked.

Dolores rolled her eyes.

Then Judy opened her eyes, smiled, turned to Dolores, seated at her left, and said, "I'd like for each of us to share what we envision when we hear the words 'Christian education.' Why don't you begin, Dolores."

"Well, it means we got to get our high-school and college graduates a Bible for Graduation Sunday, which is the end of this month. Who's graduating this year, anyway?"

Didn't I read in the *Herald* that Miriam Hodge's nephew is graduating?" Opal Majors asked.

"Yes, but they go to the Methodist church."

"That may very well be, but he's a Whicker, and they're members here."

"Why'd they leave?" Frank asked.

"It was back when Pastor Taylor was here," Opal explained. "Howard Whicker wanted to be an usher, but the church voted in Asa Peacock instead."

"I wasn't aware we voted for ushers," I said.

"We don't anymore," Dolores explained. "Howard was our biggest giver. We took a real hit when he left."

"Maybe if we gave his son a graduation Bible, he'd come back,"

Opal said. "We sure could use the money."

This wasn't turning into the meaningful conversation Judy Iverson had hoped for. "How about you, Opal?" she asked. "What do you think of when you hear the words 'Christian education'?"

"It makes me think of Donut Sunday."

Ever since God was a child, the Christian Education Committee has served donuts and coffee before Sunday school on the last Sunday of each month.

Judy smiled pleasantly. "I see. So you think of fellowship and communing with one another."

"No, I was thinking that the Kroger is having a donut sale, so maybe we oughta buy a year's supply and store 'em in the freezer."

Judy Iverson closed her eyes, envisioned a mountain meadow, then breathed out, releasing all her destructive ideas about Opal.

She tried a different tack. "Perhaps we could look at the new curriculum I had in mind." She began distributing it around the table.

"What's wrong with the old curriculum?" Dolores asked.

Judy smiled. "I thought it would be nice to change things a little bit."

Opal Majors looked at Judy as if she'd suggested they shave their heads, pierce their tongues, and convert to Buddhism.

Dolores Hinshaw read the table of contents, scowling. "I hope you don't expect the church to pay for this nonsense?"

"I thought we could take it out of our committee budget," Judy explained.

"Then we won't be able to afford donuts," Opal Majors complained.

Judy volunteered to make coffee cake for Donut Sundays.

"Then we couldn't very well call it Donut Sunday if we served coffee cake, now could we?" Opal said.

It went like that for the rest of the meeting—Judy pitched ideas, and Dolores and Opal took turns swatting them down. "No!" to the new curriculum, "No!" to coffee cake, "No!" to replacing Alice Stout, and "Most certainly not!" to Judy teaching a class on world religions.

I decided to do an end run around the Christian Education Committee. If they wouldn't ask Alice Stout to resign, perhaps I could talk her into stepping aside. So the next day I drove to the nursing home in Cartersburg. When I arrived, Alice was having one of her more lucid moments, which meant she was aware of her surroundings and not happy about it. "Who stuck me in this dump? It smells like an outhouse. Take me home."

Then her train derailed, and she squinted her eyes, inspecting me. "Who are you?"

"I'm Sam Gardner, your pastor."

"Where do I go to church?"

"Harmony Friends. Remember?"

"Never heard of it."

She picked at her lap robe.

I asked if I could pray for her. She bowed her head instinctively. I thanked God for her life, and her ministry at Harmony Friends Meeting. I prayed she would know God's peace, then said "Amen." I looked up to find her staring out the window as if she were looking for yesterday, but couldn't find it.

I patted her hand good-bye, then drove to Judy Iverson's house and told her if she taught my young adult class, I'd teach the elementary class with Alice Stout, which Judy agreed to do.

That Sunday, I arrived at church earlier than usual, turned on the lights, started the coffee, and set out the bulletins on the table at the front door. Then I carried the big pulpit chair downstairs to the elementary classroom. It was actually a bishop's chair. We'd purchased it in 1892 from the Episcopalians after they'd folded their tents and left town. I'd never cared for it and had always sat in the smaller chair next to it.

When Alice tottered into the room on her walker, I helped her to the bishop's chair and eased her down in it. She bounced up and down slightly, testing the softness.

"You've been promoted," I told her. "You are the Sunday School Queen."

She seemed intrigued with the notion. "I always wanted to be a queen," she said.

"Well, now you are."

My sons came in, Levi and Addison, and the Grant boys, and Dale and Dolores Hinshaw's two granddaughters, who were visiting for the weekend.

I took the roll, passed the basket for Brother Norman's shoe ministry to the Choctaw Indians, and then asked Alice Stout to lead us in prayer. You can never be sure what year Alice might be living in. This Sunday it was 1961, and she prayed for President Kennedy to stand strong in the face of Communist aggression.

The lesson was about Jonah, which is not an easy story to teach impressionable children, and Alice wasn't much help.

"Did Jonah really get swallowed by a fish?" my son Addison asked.

"You bet your bippee, he did," Alice said. "You can't run from God. He'll hunt you down and nail your hide to the wall, if He's a mind to."

"He's kinda like Superman, except He has a beard and He's a lot older," Billy Grant explained to Addison.

"Not exactly," I said. "But that's not the important part of the story anyway. The important thing is that God loved the Ninevites and sent Jonah to help them."

"Who were the Ninevites?" Addison asked.

"A bunch of perverts, if you ask me," Alice said. "The Lord sent two angels to warn them, and the men of the city went mad with lust."

"I believe you're thinking of Sodom and Gomorrah," I pointed out to Alice.

"Ninevites, Sodomites, Gomorites. What's the difference?" she said. "They all needed killing, if you ask me."

And people wonder why pastors burn out at an alarming rate.

I tried to wrap up the lesson. "Let's just remember that God taught Jonah an important lesson about loving your enemies."

"The thing about Ninevites, you lop off one or two of their heads, and the rest of 'em fall in line pretty quick," Alice declared.

Being crowned Sunday School Queen appeared to bring out the worst in her.

Hoping to redeem the lesson, I asked the children if they had any enemies they could love.

"How about the Russians?" Billy Grant asked.

I explained that the Russians weren't our enemies anymore.

"Bullfeathers," Alice said, turning toward Billy. "Don't ever trust a Commie, son. They'd sooner slit your throat than look at you."

The sad thing was, Alice Stout with her mind gone was not much different than who she was when she'd been in full possession of it.

Sometimes I wish I were the kind of pastor who challenged unkind behavior. Mostly I just complain about it to my wife. The upside of my timidity is job security. The downside is that my church's idea of suffering for the sake of righteousness is eating coffee cake instead of donuts.

On a more positive note, we were probably the only church in America that had a Sunday School Queen.

T h r e e

The Drill

The Dairy Queen opened late this year, fueling speculation about the owners, Oscar and Livinia Purdy, and the reason for the delay. Kyle Weathers, over at the barbershop, had heard Oscar was near death in a hospital in Pensacola, Florida, where they winter.

"Near as I can tell, it's the West Nile virus," Kyle told Bob Miles, who had been casting about for a headline for that week's edition of the *Harmony Herald*. The traditional headline for the first week of May was the opening of the Dairy Queen, with free sprinkles on every cone. But with the opening delayed, Bob was desperate for hard news.

West Nile Virus Strikes Local Citizen! he wrote in that week's *Herald*. This hearsay could have been laid to rest if the Purdys' son, Myron, had been in town, but he had left the day before on a week-long fishing trip after his mother had phoned to tell him their car was in the shop and that they wouldn't be home until the next week. With no one in town to squelch the rumor, it became hard news by Friday morning, and by Friday afternoon Oscar was pronounced dead. The Coffee Cup was abuzz with the news on Saturday morning.

"What more do you know?" Asa Peacock asked Bob Miles.

Bob didn't know much, but felt free to fill in the blank spots with some theories of his own.

"Mostly, what we know is that he was near death in the hospital with the West Nile virus. And now they're saying he's not there. No one's heard from them. What else could it be? He's dead, I tell you. Now Myron's gone and so is his truck. We think he's on his way to Florida to be with his mother," Bob conjectured.

There is a vigorous funeral industry in Harmony, which kicked into gear with the news of Oscar's passing. Though Oscar and Livinia are not churchgoers, it was recalled that Oscar's mother had belonged to Harmony Friends Meeting, so it fell to me to preach Oscar's funeral. My phone had been ringing off the hook with people wanting details. I explained to the callers that I didn't know much; I hadn't actually spoken with the widow, but if they wanted to help, I knew Livinia could use their prayers and that donations of food for the Purdy family could be left at our meetinghouse.

Down at the funeral home, floral arrangements began arriving for Oscar's funeral. Johnny Mackey wasn't even aware he'd died, but, as he told his wife, he was often the last to know these things. He stored the flowers in his cooler and began notifying all concerned about Oscar's tragic demise.

Oscar had grown up in Cartersburg, the county seat. Johnny phoned the paper there with details for the obituary and set the funeral for next Wednesday, after Bob Miles explained to him that Myron had gone to Florida to bring his father's body home.

As for Oscar and Livinia, their car was now fixed, and they were enjoying a leisurely drive home on the Blue Ridge Parkway, which they'd been wanting to do for several years. The interstates made them nervous, with the trucks hurtling past, squeezing them off the road. Though it took longer to get home, driving on the parkway was more agreeable.

They phoned Myron on Sunday evening to tell him they wouldn't be home until the middle of the week, but there was no answer.

"Maybe he's on a date," Livinia said hopefully.

"I bet that's it," Oscar said, though he thought it unlikely. Myron's dating opportunities had never been numerous.

They tried once again, around eleven o'clock. They let it ring a dozen times before hanging up.

"Must have been some date," said Oscar.

The next day found them in North Carolina. The mountain laurels were in bloom. They stopped at scenic overlooks to take pictures.

"We shoulda done this a long time ago," Oscar said. "This is somethin' else."

"We always had to get back to the Dairy Queen," Livinia pointed out.

Back at the Dairy Queen, bouquets of flowers were piled along the west wall, where Oscar had sat in his lawn chair on summer afternoons, watching the traffic go past on Highway 36.

Down the street at the meetinghouse, I was seated at my desk, writing the eulogy for Oscar's funeral. I normally liked to meet with the family prior to writing the eulogy, but with Livinia and

Myron out of town it wasn't possible. I tried not to think how grief-stricken they must be.

I had known Oscar all my life, so thinking up something to say about him wasn't difficult. He had been my coach in Little League. After the games he would drive us to the Dairy Queen in the back of his pickup truck and give us Dilly Bars. On summer afternoons when I was a child, I'd ride my bike up to the Dairy Queen and visit with Oscar. If I stopped by at closing time, he would let me have the leftover ice cream from the ice-cream freezers before he took them apart to clean them. In my fourteenth summer, I gained twenty-five pounds.

I'd invited Oscar and Livinia to church several times, but they'd never come. Dale Hinshaw liked to use Oscar as an example in his men's Sunday school class. "Now take Oscar Purdy, for instance. He's one of the nicest guys in this town, but when the Day of Judgment comes, do you think that's gonna matter one bit to the Lord. Not a bit. He's gonna look at Oscar and see pure sin and send him to hell just as quick as He would Hitler. So if you think you can get to heaven just cause you're a nice guy, then you better think again, mister."

I was glad Dale wasn't preaching Oscar's eulogy. To Dale a funeral wasn't a funeral unless the pastor hauled an unsaved sinner by the scruff of his neck down front to the casket to give him a glimpse of his fate. I'm not sure what made Dale this way. His wife once hinted that Dale's father was a hard and cruel man. It's been said people's notion of God has much to do with how their parents treated them, which might explain why Dale's God is prone to whapping people upside the head.

The fact that Oscar didn't belong to our church didn't keep the Friendly Women's Circle from gathering in the meetinghouse kitchen on Tuesday morning to make meat loaf for the funeral dinner. Fern Hampton was stirring oatmeal, ketchup, and onions into the ground beef, while lamenting the consequences of Oscar's passing. "He used to donate Dilly Bar sticks for Sunday school crafts. Now we're gonna have to buy them."

The other women weren't sure whether it was the onions or the prospect of having to spend five dollars for Dilly Bar sticks that was causing Fern to tear up.

"It's always the little things you miss about a person when they're gone," Bea Majors observed, her voice catching.

"I'm just thinking of poor Livinia," Jessie Peacock said. "Can you imagine how dreadful it would be to have your husband die and you're all alone a thousand miles from home?"

"I saw a movie about that once," Opal Majors said. "This woman's car broke down on a deserted highway in the middle of the night and she got abducted by a motorcycle gang, and then they . . . well, I'd rather not say what they did. But you know those motorcycle people."

"Clevis Nagle has a motorcycle, and he's an usher in the church," Miriam Hodge pointed out.

"I never did like that man," Fern Hampton said. "And that chippy little daughter of his, runnin' off to Hollywood and dancin' in that underwear commercial. She oughta be ashamed of herself."

"She brought a green-bean casserole for the funeral dinner," Jessie Peacock said. "She must not be all that bad."

"One green-bean casserole doesn't make up for a life of perversion," Fern declared.

That afternoon at the funeral home, Johnny Mackey and I were going over Oscar's funeral plans. "He made prearrangements just last fall before they left for Florida. Said he didn't want Livinia to have to worry about these things. It's as if he knew he wasn't gonna make it back."

I shook my head at the mystery of it.

Johnny studied the card he'd filled out on Oscar. "Hmm, that's interesting. Says here he wants to be cremated and have his ashes scattered on the Little League diamond."

"He always did have a flair for the dramatic."

"Don't forget we have to pick out hymns too," Johnny said. "Are there any hymns about baseball or ice cream?"

"Not that I'm aware of. The church tends to confine its subject matter to God."

"How about 'Take Me Out to the Ball Game'?" Johnny suggested. "It sounds real nice on the organ at the ball park."

"That's probably not appropriate for a funeral. I was thinking of something a bit more dignified."

"Yeah, you're probably right. How about 'Now Thank We All Our God'? I always did like that song."

"I don't think so," I said. "That makes it sound like we're glad Oscar died."

"Guess I hadn't thought of it that way," Johnny conceded. "I suppose you're right."

We picked three hymns, then phoned the organist, Bea Majors, to report our choices. Not that it mattered. When Bea played the organ, everything sounded alike anyway.

Wednesday morning, the day of the funeral, found Oscar and Livinia in Cincinnati, Ohio, eating breakfast at their hotel restaurant. Oscar was poring over his roadmap. "At this rate, we'll roll into town a little after ten."

"I'm almost dreading it," Livinia said. "It'll be work, work, work getting the Dairy Queen opened up. It makes me want to keep on driving."

"We gotta go home sometime. We're late as it is."

Coincidentally, that's the same thing I was thinking. "Where are they with his ashes?" I asked Johnny Mackey. "Has Livinia or Myron even bothered to phone you?"

"Actually, I haven't talked with either one of them yet. I've been working with Bob Miles."

"Well, that's just fine," I said. "What if they don't show up? What if Oscar's late for his own funeral?"

"That would be a first for me," Johnny said. "Folks have generally been real good about showing up for their funerals."

At nine-thirty, the funeral home began filling with mourners. With no widow to comfort, they were at a loss for what to do. Johnny and I huddled in his office, where I suggested we postpone the funeral until the deceased and his widow could be present.

"We can't do that," Johnny said. "These people came here expecting a funeral and we have to give them one."

So at ten o'clock Bea faded her organ playing to an end, and Johnny Mackey gave me the high sign to begin Oscar's service.

As eulogies go, it was a touching one. My voice trembled in all the right places. By the end of my tribute, even the people who'd never much cared for Oscar were dabbing their eyes.

With no ashes to spread, I invited everyone to join us for the funeral dinner in the meetinghouse basement. People began heading to their cars and were clustered in front of the funeral home when Oscar and Livinia drove past. Oscar bumped the car horn, and Livinia waved to all their friends, who seemed rather puzzled.

"Wonder who died?" Oscar asked.

"I bet it was Thelma Darnell," Livinia said. "Remember? Myron mentioned in his phone call last week that her family had taken her to the hospital."

"Oh, that's right. I wished we'd known. We could've sent flowers."

"I'll cook something tonight and take it over to them," Livinia said.

Back at the funeral home, we weren't as happy as we should have been. "Would you look at that," Fern Hampton grumped. "He didn't even bother coming to his own funeral. How disrespectful can you get."

"Looks like I bought a new suit for nothing," Asa Peacock commented to Jessie.

Bob Miles was ecstatic. What a headline this'll make, he thought. *Local Man Comes Back from the Dead!!*

When people fail to do anything newsworthy, the successful journalist must create news, which is how Bob has lasted. What an exhilarating week he'd had! Two magnificent headlines, a half-page obituary, and a copy of my eulogy in his suit pocket, just in time for this week's *Herald*.

All in all, people took it well. If schools had fire drills and the armies had battle drills, it was probably prudent for a town to have an occasional funeral drill. We talked about it during the funeral meal in the meetinghouse basement.

"That was a fine job you did," Ellis Hodge told me, patting me on the back. "You had me reaching for my hankie a time or two. I'm just sorry Oscar and Livinia weren't there to hear it."

"Never hurts to practice," I said.

"I suppose you're right," Ellis agreed.

The meat loaf was superb—moist and flavorful. The Friendly Women looked on from the kitchen, beaming.

There were several who commented that it has been the finest funeral the town had seen since Juanita Harmon's death by stove explosion in 1967. Fine enough to make several persons wish they could expire while the town's bereavement abilities were at their peak.

f o u r

Home

When my wife and I had agreed to purchase Dr. Neely's ances-
tral home, we had been so taken with the oak trees, brick sidewalks,
and porches, we'd failed to notice the flaking paint and the rotten
eaves. I don't do well with heights, but I had, with a little prodding
from my wife, been scraping and painting the lower half of the
house for the past year whenever I've had a spare moment.

Around the middle of May, I turned my attention to the eaves.
I borrowed a ladder from my father and inched my way upward,
clinging to the rungs with a white-knuckled grip. I hoped if I
could build up enough layers of paint on the wood, I might not
have to replace it.

When I reached the second-story window, my knees began to
tremble and I felt dizzy. Barbara was standing at the base of the ladder, holding a sofa cushion in the event I fell, which was looking
more probable every moment.

"Why don't we hire someone to do this?" she yelled up from the
ground.

"I can do it myself," I shouted back.

It would stagger the mind to know how many men in Harmony have perished while saying, "I can do it myself"—that brief, seemingly harmless declaration, followed by an explosion or anguished scream or severed limb.

I peered at the wood sill beneath the window. It looked spongy. I pulled a screwdriver from my back pocket and began probing. The screwdriver sank in up to its hilt.

"Remind me to replace this piece," I called down to Barbara.

"Do you know how to do that?"

"No, but I can read a book about it."

My books on home repairs are a source of merriment to the other men in town, who consider directions an affront to their masculinity. These men also believe it's immoral to hire someone to work on their houses so long as they can stand erect. Consequently, most of the houses in town are monuments to the half-finished project.

Two winters before, Bill Muldock's roof had sprung a leak. He'd covered the entire roof with blue plastic sheets until the weather was warm enough to reshingle the roof, which he still hasn't gotten around to doing. Kyle Weathers is his neighbor and thought about complaining to Bill, but then he'd have had to fill in the hole in his own yard from when the sewer pipe had burst the year before.

Bill had read in a magazine about a new type of roofing material that can be sprayed on using a garden hose, and he's waiting for Uly Grant to order it in at the hardware store. Kyle isn't filling in the hole because he's been thinking of putting in an ornamental pond in that very spot, just as soon as he has time.

I would be the same way if Barbara didn't step in and finish the jobs I'd started. As a result, she is well versed in home repair and can often be seen in Grant's Hardware buying plumbing innards and various tools. I hear about it whenever I visit the Coffee Cup.

"Say, Sam, I saw your wife buying duct tape last week. What'd you mess up this time?"

After painting the first level of our home, I decided it would be less embarrassing to hire Ernie Matthews to finish the job than it would be for the Coffee Cup men to drive past, see my wife perched on the ladder, paintbrush in hand, and taunt me for the remainder of my life.

So in late May I stopped by Ernie's house. I'd never been inside Ernie's house before, and seeing it in person didn't increase my confidence in his abilities. The screen was torn out of the front door and the floor of the porch was rotted through. Even before I crossed the porch, I detected an unpleasant odor. I knocked on the door.

"Who is it?" Ernie yelled from inside the house.

"It's me, Sam Gardner."

"Oh, come on in, Sam. But watch where you step. Haven't had time to clean things up this week."

From the looks of it, Ernie hadn't had time to clean things up for several years. Cages were stacked around the living room and kitchen. Ernie was seated on the couch, wedged between two cages, a TV remote control in his hand, which he was jabbing vigorously in the direction of the television.

"Hey, Sam."

"Hi, Ernie," I said in a strained voice, trying not to breathe.

"What's up?"

"Just wanted to know if you could maybe paint the top half of my house."

"I'm not doing much painting these days," Ernie said. "Been too busy." He continued working the remote control, cycling through the stations. "I'm in the ferret business. Wanna buy a ferret?"

"Not right now," I said. "Maybe later."

"So how come you just want the top half of your house painted?" Ernie asked.

"Uh, well, I did the bottom part myself. But I'm not so good on ladders."

Ernie thought for a moment, then looked around, surveying his ferrets. "I got my hands full here, what with all my corporate interests, but maybe I could finish paintin' your house. But I got to warn you, I sent Oprah a picture of me and my ferrets and if she calls and wants us on her show, we're off to Hollywood."

"I'm willing to take that chance. Could you start tomorrow?"

"Don't see why not."

The next morning, Ernie still hadn't arrived by the time I was ready to leave for work. "Have him start on the front of the house first," I told Barbara. At any given time, Ernie was painting three or four houses in town, moving from one to the other as the mood struck him. If he painted the front first, it would look nice from the street for the remaining two months it took him to finish the job.

I phoned at noon to see if Ernie had started.

"He's here," Barbara reported. "And I told him to start on the front of the house, just like you said. But something doesn't look

34

quite right. Maybe you ought to come home."

It's a three-block walk from the meetinghouse to home, which I covered in just under two minutes. My wife was standing on the sidewalk, her hands on her hips, inspecting the house from a variety of angles.

"That doesn't look like the right color," she said as I approached. "What do you think?"

I studied our home. "I think you're right. Hey, Ernie, what color of paint is that?"

"Eggshell."

I groaned. "That's the wrong color. I told you ecru."

Ernie climbed down the ladder. "I had some eggshell left over from Hester Gladden's house. With all the trees in your front yard, people won't be able to tell the difference."

"I can tell the difference," my wife yelled from the sidewalk.

I was in a predicament. If I made Ernie mad, he'd pack his paintbrushes and leave. Still, I didn't think it was asking too much for Ernie to paint the upper half of our house the same color as the lower half. I lowered my voice conspiratorially, draped my arm around Ernie, and steered him out of earshot of my wife. "Personally, Ernie, I think it looks just fine. But you know how picky women can be."

"Don't I know it," Ernie said.

Ernie is forty-two and has never been married, due to the pickiness of women, who for some reason don't feel romantically inclined toward a man who never shaves his neck.

"Darn women," Ernie said.

"You got that right."

Now it was us guys standing united against the women of the world. I was halfway home. "We're probably better off just painting it the way she wants it."

Ernie glanced at Barbara. "Yeah, I suppose you're right."

With the crisis averted, I went in the house for lunch. A grilled cheese and tomato soup with peaches in heavy syrup. My favorite.

By one o'clock I was back at my desk, working on my sermon. People haven't been listening as closely to my sermons as they once did. They appear bored. The month before, I had purchased a new book on the writing and delivery of sermons called *From Humdrum to Hallelujah!* The first chapter concerned itself with the appropriate facial expressions a pastor should employ while preaching. The author advised keeping the eyebrows raised throughout the sermon to convey enthusiasm, the idea being that the congregation won't be enthusiastic if the minister isn't.

The next Sunday, I kept my eyebrows raised during the entire sermon, but only succeeded in giving myself a headache.

On the walk home, Barbara asked me if anything was wrong with me during my sermon.

"I was trying to appear enthusiastic," I said.

"You looked alarmed, like you had to use the bathroom."

The book also suggested working personal anecdotes into the sermon that revealed the pastor's frailties. So while preaching on the text, "Lead us not into temptation, but deliver us from evil," I confessed my struggle with lust.

Fortunately for me, no one was paying attention except my wife, whose job it is to look enthralled with my every public utterance.

But she was less than enthralled with my confession and for the next several days grilled me on the object of my lust. When I said it was her, she snorted. "That shows what you know," she said. "You can't lust after your own spouse."

"You most certainly can." I'd looked up the word in the dictionary. "*Lust* means to have an intense desire or need for someone or something. Why can't I have an intense desire or need for you?"

That mollified her somewhat. The next day I gave *From Humdrum to Hallelujah!* to Pastor Jimmy of the Harmony Worship Center, hoping it would make his life as miserable as it had my own.

This is our fourth year back home. All things considered, it's been a good move. I like it because I have to be only slightly better than the other men in town, and the competition is not very stiff. As long as my neck is shaved and I refrain from wearing a seed-corn cap, I'm head and shoulders above the crowd.

It occurs to me that most of the people in town are content with the humdrum. If they wanted hallelujah, they'd live someplace where excellence isn't suspect. Ernie Matthews is right. No one would have noticed if our house had been painted two colors. It's the same way with my sermons. If they're bad, I'm the only one who notices. Everyone still shakes my hand and says, "Nice sermon, Pastor," whether it was or not.

Ernie finished painting our house on a Friday, after an unusually quick two weeks. That evening, we stood out front underneath the oak trees marveling at our home. There are few moments as pleasant as surveying your freshly painted house, knowing you're good for another ten years.

"Isn't it beautiful?" I said.

"It looks very nice," my wife agreed. "Ernie did a good job."

"Don't forget that I painted the bottom half."

"I haven't forgotten. I still haven't scraped all the paint off the windows."

We walked up the sidewalk to the porch and sat down on the swing, rocking back and forth, enjoying a slight breeze from the west, watching our boys play baseball in the side yard.

"Sometimes," I said, "I catch myself thinking of the boys being grown and gone away and it being just you and I rattling around in this old house."

"You like that feeling?"

"I do," I said. "I really do."

We continued to swing in a companionable silence.

"I hope the boys don't move too far away," Barbara said after a while.

"Maybe just far enough away to meet some nice girls and get married," I said. "Then they can move back here and start having babies and help me paint the house."

Barbara laughed. She reached over and took my hand. "You know what I love about you?"

"My rugged good looks?"

"Besides that."

"I give up. What?"

"A lot of men would never admit they were too scared to get up on a ladder and paint their house, but not you."

"It's not that I was afraid to do it, or that I couldn't do it," I explained. "I just knew Ernie needed the work. I did it to help Ernie."

"That's another thing I love about you. You're always thinking of other people."

"Thank you," I said.

"It isn't always easy to point to a particular instance and say, "That was the moment our house became our home." But I knew this was such a time—sitting on the porch swing, my arm around my beloved, whom I intensely desired and needed, listening to the slap of a ball in a baseball mitt.

"Now all we need is a new roof," Barbara said.

"Funny you should mention that. Bill Muldock told me about something you can spray on your roof that keeps you from having to replace it. He read about it in a magazine."

My wife sighed.

Yes, this was the moment, I thought. Fully aware of my home's every blemish, but loving it just the same.

f i v e

The Gift

*I*t was early in June, and the church was holding its annual meeting to decide whether they'd keep me on another year. Theoretically, we were to wait quietly upon the Lord to discern His will in the matter. But the way it really worked was that I could keep the job so long as I didn't annoy a majority of the congregation. Dale Hinshaw wanted to know where I stood on the evolution issue and suggested I was derelict in my duties for not preaching about hell. Miriam Hodge gave him his customary five minutes to rant before announcing it was the Lord's will for me to stay. The congregation rumbled their approval and, with that, I was on the payroll for another year.

The next day was Friday, my sermon-writing day. When Frank arrived, I was seated at my desk, joining paper clips into a length while quibbling on the phone with my wife about where to have lunch. We meet for lunch every Friday. It's our standing date, our ongoing effort to keep the marital flame ablaze. So far all it's done is provide one more thing to argue about, namely, where to dine. I prefer hamburgers and onion rings from the Coffee Cup, while Barbara is fond of tuna-salad croissants with pasta salad and a fruit cup at the Legal Grounds Coffee Shop.

"How can you stand that place?" she said. "It's so greasy. They'd fry the orange juice if they could figure out a way."

A week before, the Coffee Cup had caught fire after Vinny tried dousing a match by immersing it in dishwater. It was the first time the fire department had ever been called to put out a sink. It was that greasy.

"It's the same old people talking about the same old things," she said. "You don't even like some of them. Why do you keep going there?"

I like to think that eating at the Coffee Cup is my way of heeding Christ's call to make disciples of all nations. Men not known for their spiritual prowess stop past my table to solicit my opinion on certain religious matters, like whether their sister's pastor, who says people are only saved if they've been baptized in the name of Jesus, is full of beans.

"Maybe you know her minister," they say. "He pastors over in Ohio."

It puzzles me why people think I know every minister in a three-state radius.

Occasionally, someone will accost me while I'm eating lunch. When Kyle Weathers's cousin had a minister in Alabama who left his wife and kids to run off with the church organist, I was a handy target. "What is it with you ministers anyway? Standing up there tellin' the rest of us what to do, then pullin' a stunt like that," Kyle complained. "You oughta be ashamed of yourself."

I apologized on behalf of all ministers everywhere, then returned to my hamburger and onion rings.

But every now and then, an opportunity will arise for me to minister. Like when Vernley Stout, the bank president, had to have a double knee replacement, and he asked me to pray for him. Vernley was eating a triple cheeseburger and drinking a milkshake, while pondering aloud why God had caused his knees to go bad. It was all I could do not to point out that Vernley's being a hundred pounds overweight might have had something to do with it. Instead, I prayed for Vernley and even drove to the hospital in the city to visit him.

Seeing Vernley writhing in the hospital bed, twisting in pain, with Frankenstein stitches down both knees, deepened my appreciation for tuna-salad croissants with pasta salad and a fruit cup. So I gave in and took my wife to the Legal Grounds for lunch.

"Now isn't this better than the Coffee Cup?" Barbara said, as she speared a chunk of watermelon from her fruit cup.

It was better, if only because being in the same room as Deena Morrison, the owner of the Legal Grounds, was far more appealing than spending my lunch hour with the mechanics from Harvey Muldock's garage. Of course, I couldn't tell my wife that, so instead I said, "Yes, and I don't feel greasy like I do after I've been to the Coffee Cup."

"Exactly," she agreed.

I finished my fruit cup, left a dollar tip for Deena, kissed my wife good-bye, then walked back to the meetinghouse office.

It was one of those early summer days a person would have to work hard to ruin. Which isn't impossible, of course, as some people have a knack for spoiling perfectly fine days. People who, when they reached heaven, would complain that the light hurt their eyes and ask God to dim His radiance, and while He was at it, could He please tell the cherubim and seraphim to pipe down, for crying out loud.

But my day was remarkably free of such people. Even Frank was in a pleasant mood when I arrived back at the meetinghouse.

He congratulated me for keeping my job another year, then told me to close my eyes, that he had a surprise for me.

"You're not going to kiss me, are you?"

"Of course not."

I heard him rise from his desk, open the closet door, then grunt. "Okay, you can open your eyes."

There was a large box on Frank's desk, tied shut with string. Small holes were cut in the top of the box. I heard a slight rustle.

"Well, go ahead, open it up," Frank said.

I untied the string and peered in the box. Two black eyes peered back. I saw a flash of white teeth and heard a snarling sound.

"Whatever it is, it's growling at me. Does it bite?"

"It might at first, but probably not after it gets to know you."

"What exactly is it?" I asked.

"A ferret."

"Oh."

I continued to look in the box. "Well, Frank," I said after a while, "I don't know what to say."

Frank beamed. "I knew you'd like it. I got it from Ernie Matthews. Did you know he raises them?"

"Yes, I had heard something about that."

"Well, I thought you and your boys might enjoy it."

"I'm sure we will." I knew I had to choose my next words carefully, so I thought for a moment, then said, "But Frank, you're the one who'd probably like the company. If you want to keep it for yourself, I certainly wouldn't blame you."

"Nope, having a pet isn't for me. I want my freedom. Oh, by the way, he'll need a cage so he doesn't chew on the furniture. I think they sell them over at the hardware store. And Ernie told me they'll spray if you don't get 'em neutered."

I nodded. "Well, it's good to know those things, I guess."

"Oh, one more thing. You have to be careful what you feed them. They're prone to diarrhea. Other than that, they're real low maintenance."

"I guess I better this little guy home," I said.

I picked up the box, held it at arm's length, and loaded the ferret in the backseat of my car. It was scrambling around inside the box, scratching to get out.

First, a cage, I thought.

I drove to Grant's Hardware. Uly Grant was standing behind the counter with his son, Billy.

"Hey, Uly. Hi, Billy. How are you, buddy?"

"Fine, except I have head lice," Billy said, just as I reached down to rub his head.

I drew my hand back. "Sorry to hear that, Billy."

"That's okay. Today's my birthday."

A thought passed through my mind. "Twelve, right?"

"Yep."

"Say, Billy, I've brought you a birthday present. But you and your daddy will need to come out to the car."

Billy grinned. Uly came out from around the counter. "Sam, this is awful nice of you. How'd you know it was his birthday."

"Uh, it's in the church calendar. Remember?"

"Oh, that's right."

We walked through the door to my car. "It's right here in the backseat, in the box."

I slid the box across the seat, placed it on the sidewalk, and opened the lid. The ferret poked its head out of the box.

"Oh, boy, a rat!" said Billy, thoroughly pleased.

"Not exactly," I said. "It's a ferret."

To say Uly was thrilled was a stretch, but it was Billy's birthday, and their dog had just died, so he kept quiet.

"You'll love it too," I told Uly. "They're a lot of fun. Very gentle animals."

"I thought I heard where a lady over in Cartersburg got attacked by one and it bit her nose off," Uly said.

"That was an urban legend," I said. "It never happened. These little guys are gentle as lambs." I reached out to stroke the ferret's head. A low snarl rose from it's throat and the fur on its neck stood up. I snatched back my hand. "They do get a little cranky when they're hungry, though."

Uly looked skeptical. "Well, I suppose we can keep it. Billy, what do you say?"

"Thank you, Mr. Gardner." He reached up and gave me a hug,

which was all it took to give me head lice, though it took several days for me to notice.

Frank was waiting when I came into the office the next morning. "So how'd the boys like it? What'd you name it?"

I thought quickly. "Furhead," I said. "Furhead the Ferret. And the boys love it."

Then I changed the subject.

The next day I began itching in earnest. I asked Barbara if she noticed a rash on my head. She parted my hair to observe my scalp, then recoiled. "Lice!" she shrieked. "You've got head lice!" She ran to the bathroom to wash her hands. "Get out of the house and don't come back inside," she yelled from the bathroom. "Go get a haircut."

The last time I'd had a burr haircut was in the first grade. Ever since then I'd worn it just off the collar. So when I came home from Kyle's barbershop shorn like a sheep and smelling most unpleasant, Barbara and the boys were beset with curiosity.

Levi sniffed around me. "What'd they put on you, Daddy?"

"Kerosene," I said glumly. "I have to keep it in my hair for twenty-four hours."

"Back away from your father, honey," Barbara warned Levi. "You," she said, pointing at me, "are sleeping in the garage tonight."

I felt like a leper, with open sores oozing pus. My penance, I thought, for unloading the ferret on Billy Grant and lying to Frank. Still, it wasn't all that bad in the garage. It was not unlike being a monk—a deep sense of guilt, coupled with a bad haircut and an uncomfortable place to sleep. Now I knew why monks got up early.

When I woke the next morning, I considered phoning in sick to church, but figured I'd lied enough lately, so I put on my good clothes and walked with my family to meeting for worship.

A few people mentioned my hair. Dale Hinshaw was positively gleeful. He thought my burr haircut signaled a theological shift, that I was giving up my liberal ways and getting serious about obeying the Word, specifically 1 Corinthians 11:14: "Does not nature itself teach you that for a man to wear long hair is degrading to him." Dale was so pleased with my conversion, I didn't have the heart to tell him it was head lice.

Frank was standing in the entryway, passing out the bulletins. He bent down to Levi. "Say, little man, how's ol' Furhead getting along?"

Levi looked puzzled, then it occurred to him Frank was probably talking about me, whose hair did, in fact, appear rather furry.

Levi laughed. "Fine, but Mom made him sleep in the garage last night."

"Don't you have a cage for him?" Frank asked.

"Nope, just the garage. But Mom said he could come in the house once he takes a bath and gets the smell out."

"Well, sure, that makes sense." Frank reached in his pocket. "Here, I brought a carrot for you to give him."

"I'm not sure he likes carrots. He doesn't eat many vegetables."

"What does he like?" Frank asked.

Levi thought for a moment. "Well, this morning for breakfast he had Cocoa Krispies."

"Are you sure that's good for him?"

P H I L I P   G U L L E Y

"Mom said he was gonna get fat, eating like that. She fixed him oatmeal, but he wouldn't eat it."

"I didn't know he was that picky," Frank said.

"Mom said it's like having another kid."

"Gee, I hope he's not too much trouble. I suppose if you want he can come live with me."

"No, we like having him."

"Well, okay then." Frank leaned closer to Levi and whispered in his ear, "But you tell your Dad if he potties on the carpet, he can come stay with me."

Levi laughed. "Okay, you can have him if he starts doing that."

Frank rubbed Levi's hair, which was all it took to give him head lice, though it was several days before he noticed.

On Monday, Levi and Addison had their hair buzzed and their heads swabbed with kerosene. I took Tuesday off to wash all the bedding and clothing. We hung the bedding on the clothesline to dry, which occupied the boys a good part of the day, playing fort among the sheets.

Frank came to work on Wednesday sporting a burr haircut, reeking of kerosene, and appearing thoroughly miserable. It was hard to feel sorry for him.

He deserves it, I thought. If he hadn't given me that stupid ferret in the first place, we'd still have our hair.

But I didn't say that. Instead, I apologized for passing on the head lice, and even though my knees had been stiff the past few days and I worried they might need to be replaced, I invited Frank to join me for lunch at the Coffee Cup, reasoning if I was going to have an operation, it might be wise to go into it weighing a few extra pounds.

49

Six

The Fourth

*I*t was Dale Hinshaw's idea for Harmony Friends Meeting to build a float for the town's Fourth of July parade. He'd been badgering us for years to participate, but we had resisted, even when he'd pointed out that every other church in town had a float in the parade. "For cryin' out loud, the Catholics got a float and they ain't even Americans. They're Vaticans. We got foreigners in this town who'll build a float and march in the Fourth of July parade, and we won't."

That is not entirely accurate. We'd marched in the 1976 bicentennial parade dressed like the old-time Quakers who founded Harmony in 1824. My chief memory of growing up in this church was being forced to wear humiliating costumes at public pageants—a bathrobe in Christmas Nativity scenes, a bedsheet draped over my shoulder when I played Jesus at the Palm Sunday pageant, and clothes like those belonging to the man on the Quaker Oats box as I marched down Main Street in view of my friends.

Since that time, we have not had a youth group at Harmony Friends Meeting. The children in our meeting hit adolescence, get wind of some scheme by the adults that will earn them the ridicule of their peers, and promptly flee to the Methodist youth group.

For the past four years, I had labored to begin a youth group, carefully nurturing the faith of the church's young people, only to have Dale scare them off when he asked them to gather at the school flagpole on the National Day of Prayer wearing T-shirts that read *A Prayer a Day Keeps Satan Away.*

I was able to woo them back by promising Dale we could have a float in the Fourth of July parade so long as he left the youth of the meeting out of it. I had a vested interest in this. My older son, Levi, had been eyeing the Methodists, and I didn't want to give him one more reason to bolt.

It's not easy being the child of a pastor because of people like Dale. Dale believes God has called my entire family to ministry. He quizzes my sons about their beliefs and whether they've given their hearts to the Lord. When Levi had turned ten, Dale informed him he'd reached the age of accountability, and that if he died now, he'd go to hell unless he'd accepted Jesus as his Savior. He gave my son Bible tracts to place in the school rest rooms on the toilet tanks, just in case a child's appointed time to meet the Lord occurred in a bathroom stall.

Fortunately, building the Fourth of July float has distracted Dale. He formed a Float Committee—Asa Peacock, Harvey Muldock, and Ellis Hodge. At their first meeting, Ellis suggested building a replica of the meetinghouse along with a banner reading *You Have a Friend at Harmony Friends!* Asa had hoped for something a little snazzier, preferably something involving his new tractor, while Dale was pushing for a float that would convict people of their sins and bring them to their knees in humble repentance.

Dale has been spending a great deal of time at the Bible bookstore in Cartersburg surveying the merchandise. He's ordered bulk quantities of Bible tracts to distribute along the parade route. One of them is called *Why Is Mary Crying?* According to the tract, Mary is crying because Catholics are worshiping her instead of her son, and Dale believes it's time someone set the record straight.

Another tract is *Flight 581,* which tells about a couple who were on their way to Las Vegas to pursue a variety of sins and perversions, only to die in an airplane crash. Thankfully, they were seated next to a minister who was going to Las Vegas to start a new church and was able to lead them to the Lord before the plane hit the ground.

But Dale's favorite tract was called *Reverend Tremendous,* about a beloved pastor who was active in ecumenical affairs and social justice work, but forgot that he was saved by grace and not works, so went straight to hell for his efforts. Dale gave me one of those.

In mid-June, after much negotiation and compromise, the Float Committee settled on a design—a ten-foot plywood replica of our meetinghouse made by Ellis and pulled behind Asa's tractor. In what can only be described as a stunning lapse of judgment, they left it to Dale to select the Scripture for the banner. He settled on Jeremiah 26:6: *"I will make this town a curse for all the nations of the earth."*

"Don't you think that's a bit negative?" Asa asked Dale. "It's just a Fourth of July parade, after all, not a revival."

"You know, Asa," Dale said. "If you wanna tickle people's ears, that's your business. But I think it's time somebody in this town stood up for the truth."

Asa let it go, reasoning that amidst the customary chaos of the parade, no one would likely notice their float.

Harvey Muldock leads the parade in his 1951 Plymouth Cranbrook convertible, and is followed by my father, driving his 1939 Farmall Model M tractor. Then comes Harvey's brother-in-law, Bernie, the town policeman, who runs his siren, which people don't mind since it drowns out the high-school band, which follows. Behind the band is the street department in the town dump truck, then the fire department riding on the tanker, followed by the Shriners from Cartersburg on their minibikes, wearing their fezzes and weaving in and out like a braid of hair. After the Shriners, Clevis Nagle pedals his old-fashioned bicycle, with its big front wheel.

Those are the professionals. After them come the amateurs—the Little League teams, the church floats, the bowling teams from the Starlight Lanes, and a politician or two, passing out candy.

It's the same parade as the Corn and Sausage Days parade in September, except for the Sausage Queen, who sits enthroned in the backseat of Harvey's convertible, waving to her subjects.

The Fourth of July parade is held in the afternoon. Then we go home for a nap and a bite to eat. After that, we reassemble at the town park at dusk and sit in our lawn chairs on the hill above the pool to watch the fireworks, which are shot off from the center field of the Little League diamond.

When I was growing up, Huey Gladden from the street department was in charge of the fireworks. But in 1976, in a valiant attempt to play the national anthem using fireworks, while rushing from one launching tube to another, he stumbled, fell upon a tube just as a Roman candle was lifting off, and very nearly achieved orbit.

These days, Darrell Furbay, the fire chief, sets off the fireworks. Although he lacks Huey Gladden's creativity, it is a comfort to enjoy the fireworks without worrying about a fatality.

The day before the parade, my boys and I washed and waxed the tractor with my father. It's been in my front yard the past two summers, after my father gave it to me, believing it would cure me of depression. I did cheer up shortly thereafter, so I'm not discounting its curative powers.

My father and I have taken turns driving it in the parades. It was my turn this year. At first I'd resisted the idea, but then I discovered I enjoyed navigating the tractor up Main Street past the stores and knots of people, waving and throwing candy.

"Can I ride with you this year?" Addison asked, as we polished the tractor.

"I don't think so, buddy. It isn't safe. You might fall off my lap."

"You could pull me behind you in a wagon."

I thought about that for a moment. "Yes, I suppose I could do that."

I phoned Ellis Hodge that evening to see if he had a hay wagon we could borrow, which he did. Addison was elated.

Levi let out a snort. "You'll look like a dork," he said to his little brother.

"Then so will you," I pointed out. "Because you're riding with us."

He began to whine, as only an eleven-year-old can.

"No complaining," I said. "Mom promised Deena she'd help her at the coffee shop. So you're stuck with me, kid. And I'm on the tractor, which means you will be too." I said it in my "And that's that!" voice, to stifle any argument.

The morning of the Fourth, the phone rang while we were eating breakfast. It was Asa Peacock, clearly distressed. "It won't start," he said. "I've been trying for two hours to get it running, and it won't start."

"What won't start?"

"My new tractor," Asa moaned. "I called the dealer and he said the computer must be out of whack. They gotta order in some parts from Atlanta."

"Gee, Asa, I'm sorry to hear that. Can you use Ellis's tractor?"

"He's got it taken apart, workin' on it. Can you pull the church float with your tractor?"

I once heard of a mental illness that causes otherwise rational persons to occasionally behave in illogical ways. I have long suspected I suffer from this malady, for the next hour found me at Dale Hinshaw's house, hitching my 1939 Farmall Model M tractor to a hay wagon bearing a replica of our meetinghouse and draped with a banner reading, "*I will make this town a curse for all the nations of the earth.*" —*Jeremiah 26:6.*

Dale was stacking cartons of tracts inside the model. "The Catholics get this one," he said, holding up a copy of *Why Is Mary Crying?* "And the liberals get *Flight 581* or *Reverend Tremendous.* It don't matter which one."

He loaded a box on the wagon.

"What's in there?" I asked.

"Salvation suckers," he replied. "I got 'em at the Bible bookstore. They got the plan of salvation written right on 'em. See?" He held one up for me to inspect.

"Those are as big as Frisbees," I observed.

"Got to be, to get all the Bible verses on 'em."

"What are you going to do with them?" I asked.

"Throw 'em to the kids."

"I don't know, Dale. What if you hit someone in the head? They're pretty heavy."

"Better a concussion than to roast in hell."

I made the boys wear their nice clothes since we were representing the church. Levi began moaning about my choice of vocations. "How come just because you're a minister, I have to do this? Why can't I just stay home?"

"Because no one's here to watch you. Your mother's helping Deena and I'm in the parade, so that's that. Now stop complaining and get dressed."

"Okay, but I'm not handing out anything."

"That's fine. You can stay inside the float and pass things to Dale. No one'll even see you."

"You're crazy," Addison said to his brother. "This'll be fun. All our friends will see us and everything."

Levi smacked his forehead. "Well, duh. Like I really want my friends to see me riding on some dorky church float."

I had a fleeting recollection of plodding down Main Street on a donkey during the town's annual Palm Sunday pageant. I was eleven years old, Levi's age. It had been our church's turn to supply a Jesus, and the finger of fate had settled on me after it was discovered that Herbert Stout, the other boy in our church, was allergic to donkeys. The elders didn't want a Jesus with hives. So I was not without sympathy.

"No one will see you," I promised Levi. "Just stay hidden inside the float and you'll be fine."

But I could tell he wasn't pleased, and that the Methodists were looking more attractive every moment.

The parade began at the elementary school, went north on Washington Street four blocks, hooked a left onto Main Street, looped around the town square, then headed back south to the school. It was always exciting to see whether the front of the parade would bisect the rear of the parade, as it did in 1976 when everyone and their brother marched in the bicentennial parade. But this year, Harvey missed Owen Stout, our perennial town board candidate, by a good twenty yards.

Levi stayed crouched in the church on the float the whole time, handing out fistfuls of tracts to Dale, who distributed them to people who in his estimation needed saving. Addison passed out the salvation suckers, eating one for every six he gave out.

Everything was going fine until the fire department's tanker passed in front of Grant's Hardware and the engine backfired. Bystanders later said it was the farthest they had ever seen an animal leap, when Billy Grant's pet ferret, the one I'd given him, jumped from his arms and began sprinting among the Shriners. It dodged Clevis Nagle on his bicycle, scattered the Little League teams, then froze as my 1939 Farmall Model M tractor with its original steel front wheel bore down. I swerved to miss it, causing the church to slide from the float and land upside down on the street with a splintering crash. Levi, though unhurt, was lodged in the steeple, his legs opening and closing in the air like a pair of scissors. Billy Grant's ferret had scrambled up Dale's leg and was perched on his head, causing Dale to speculate that God had indeed made our town a curse for all the nations of the earth, just as Jeremiah had predicted.

This was the picture Bob Miles snapped for the front page of the *Harmony Herald*, alongside an article about Billy Grant and his pet ferret and how he'd come to own it. Bob also interviewed Dale Hinshaw, who prophesied that this was the first of many catastrophes God would visit upon our town for our sins.

"I'm never going to be in a parade again," Levi told me that night, after the fireworks.

"I said the same thing when I was your age."

"Then how come you were in the parade today?" he asked.

I thought for a moment. "Because Asa Peacock asked for my help, and he's my friend."

"Is Dale your friend?"

"I wouldn't want to go on vacation with him," I said, "but I don't wish him any harm."

A car turned in front of our house, it's headlights casting shadows against my son's bedroom wall.

"Is it always like this in the church?" Levi asked, after a while.

"Always like what?"

"You have to be with people you don't like."

"Sometimes it's like that. But there are also a lot of wonderful people."

"I'm still not going to ride on the church float ever again," he said.

"Fair enough, sport."

I lay in bed that night thinking how nothing ever changes. I'm forty-two years old and still having to do things I don't want to do. I suppose it's the price of loving people. My son thinks he'll somehow avoid these obligations, which is a common misperception among the young. In time, of course, he'll learn otherwise, that maturity isn't about doing what pleases us, but bearing with good humor that which annoys us to no end.

I forget this myself sometimes, so it's good to be reminded, lest in my arrogance I despise the Dales of the world for not marching to my tune. When I was a child, my father would advise me not to take myself so seriously. I wondered if I should wake my son to pass this truth along, then decided against it. There are some lessons we have to learn on our own, lessons whose truths aren't accepted until the soul is ready to hear them.

Seven

Freedom Month

A heat wave rolled into town the week after the Fourth and has hunkered down for a long stay. It's been the hottest July in forty-eight years, or so Bob Miles at the *Herald* noted in an editorial warning about global warming, which agitated the conservatives, causing them to fire off letters to the editor. They complain about the liberal slant of the *Herald* and how it's time true Americans stood up for their rights, which apparently includes the right to tell editors what they can and cannot publish in a newspaper. The irony of this seems to escape them, so Bob points it out in another editorial, which provokes them even further.

Civil liberties have never really caught on with some people in our town. Freedom of the press is fine, as long as the press agrees with them. These same people attend the school-board meetings demanding freedom of religion, that our children be made to pray whether they want to or not. But not just any prayer will do; it has to conform to certain theological assumptions and be led by the teacher. Unless the teacher objects, at which point the school board might reconsider why they hired that teacher in the first place.

Bob has declared July "Freedom Month" at the *Herald* in honor of America's birthday. The first week he wrote about freedom of the press. The second week he wrote that freedom of religion also included freedom from religion. This did not generate the controversy he'd hoped for, so in the third week he wrote about the freedom of association, that Americans ought to be free to associate with whomever they wished. It was one of those editorials that had the men at the Coffee Cup saying, "You got that right, mister," all the way through, until they hit the last paragraph, in which Bob contended that if we really believed in free association, then gay people ought to be free to marry one another.

The *Herald* landed on our doorsteps on Thursday afternoon. When I arrived at the meetinghouse office on Friday morning, thirteen messages were on the answering machine wanting to know if Bob Miles was a member of our church and, if so, could we boot him out or censure him or possibly burn him at the stake.

Frank nailed me as soon as I came through the door. "The ministerial association is holding an emergency meeting at ten o'clock. They asked if you could be there."

I'd been avoiding the ministerial association meetings for the past six months, ever since they'd elected Pastor Jimmy of the Harmony Worship Center as their president. I had better things to do than listen to him boast about the growth of his church. Truth be told, I think they were glad I was staying away. They'd been shunning me since the year before, when I'd suggested we hold a peace rally on the town square. The motion had failed, five to one. They had then forged boldly ahead with their plans to have a booth at the Corn and Sausage Days festival.

"Could you please call them, thank them for their invitation, but tell them I can't make it?" I asked Frank. "I need to work on my sermon."

Within the hour, Dale Hinshaw and Fern Hampton were in my office. Although I'd given Frank firm instructions to keep Dale and Fern at bay, he was upset that I'd given the ferret to Billy Grant. He retaliated by ushering into my office Dale and Fern, who demanded to know what I was going to do about Bob Miles.

"What would you suggest I do?"

"Kick him out of the church," Fern said.

I pointed out that he wasn't a member.

"So let's make him a member and then kick him out."

"What did Bob do that was so awful?"

"He's promoting filth," Dale said. "He's wreckin' the institution of marriage."

"His editorial didn't hurt my marriage. Do you know anyone who's gotten divorced because of Bob's editorial?"

But Dale had worked himself to a lather and wasn't in the mood for reason. He predicted if Bob weren't silenced, all manner of tragedies would follow, up to and including the fall of Western civilization.

"Not to mention how it'll affect the Corn and Sausage Days festival," Fern Hampton screeched. "You think God-fearing Christians will want to visit a town that's given itself over to perversion? And if that flops, so does our Chicken Noodle Dinner. And there go our chances of ever getting new kitchen cabinets. But I suppose you haven't thought about that."

They ranted on for fifteen minutes before my telephone rang. I excused myself and answered it. It was my wife, reminding me to meet her for lunch. She hung up, but I stayed on the line, feigning a pastoral emergency so I could pry Fern and Dale from my office. I looked up apologetically. "I'm afraid I need some privacy," I told them. "Thank you for stopping by."

They harrumphed in unison, turned, and stalked from my office.

The day did not improve. My phone rang continually as a variety of enraged citizens and church members called to demand I lead the battle for righteousness against Bob Miles. My only break came at lunchtime, when I met my wife at the Legal Grounds for our weekly date. It is the town's one safe haven for progressive thinkers. Deena had posted the editorial page from the *Herald* on her bulletin board just inside the door, along with a letter of support for Bob Miles, which she invited us to sign.

"No, thank you," I told Deena. "I think I'll remain above the fray."

"Not me," my wife said. "I'll sign it." And with that, she took the pen from Deena and signed her name in big, bold letters, with a flourish.

By Sunday morning, the town was locked in the grip of a civil war, with the Bob bashers far outnumbering his defenders. Meeting for worship was a disaster, with Dale praying aloud that the Lord would smite Bob, lest his sin infect the town. By then, word had gotten out that my wife had signed the letter in support of Bob. So after Dale had prayed for Bob's destruction, he waded in on me, chastising me for not making my wife submit to me, in accordance with the Scriptures.

I didn't respond, electing to follow Jesus' example of remaining silent before his accusers.

Miriam Hodge stood and pled for tolerance, which was like standing in a tavern and arguing for sobriety. Bea Majors began playing the organ to drown her out.

It was a bitter hour.

I took Monday off and went with my family on a picnic at a state park sixty miles away, where no one ever read the *Herald*. I thought of taking the week off, but was short of vacation days. Instead, I had Frank, who had since forgiven me, guard my office door, weeding out the malcontents from those sincerely needing help.

On Thursday morning, Opal Majors arrived to start pasting together the church newsletter, as she has since 1967, when Juanita Harmon met her untimely demise while lighting the meetinghouse stove. Opal agreed to do it until we could find a replacement for Juanita, and she's been at it ever since. We can't pry it from her now, as much as we'd like to. The whole newsletter is one long editorial, with the church activities and Opal's opinion of them woven together into a four-page dissertation, all of it one paragraph and single-spaced.

"Are you coming to the march?" she asked me.

"What march?"

"The march on Bob. It's this Saturday. All the churches in town are participating. It's on the flier."

"What flier?"

"From the ministerial association," she said. "It had your name on it. Didn't you read it?"

"What do you mean it had my name on it?"

"At the bottom, along with all the other ministers."

"Do you have a copy I can see?" I asked.

"Yeah, it's here somewhere," Opal said, rifling through her purse. "I got to tell you, Sam, I was real proud to see your name on it. There for a while I thought you were turning liberal on us."

She handed me the flier, and I read it. Just as I had feared, it was contemptible—a withering tirade against gays and the liberal media elite. It bore no resemblance to the gospel. And there was my name, heading the list of signatures.

"It's in today's *Herald* too," Opal said, beaming. "On the editorial page. We're awful proud of you for taking a stand, Sam."

It took an hour to find out who'd added my name to the flier— Pastor Jimmy at the Harmony Worship Center. It had been his last nefarious act before leaving town for a two-week vacation, which, in retrospect, was a blessing, as it prevented my hunting him down and taking his life.

As for Bob Miles, he was elated. Newspaper sales had never been better. He'd been back to press three times in the past week. Dale Hinshaw had purchased one hundred extra copies so he could burn them on the day of the march.

Bob had added four pages to the paper in order to print all the letters to the editor he'd received and was now selling the paper for a dollar a copy as a special edition. He'd also published his next editorial, in which he proposed the government add Bill Clinton's face to Mount Rushmore. Dale bought two hundred extra copies of that one.

By the day of the march, nearly everyone in town was against Bob. If he had written these editorials in the winter, no one would have minded. It would have provided a pleasant philosophical diversion, something to argue about good-naturedly down at the Coffee Cup. But he wrote them in the summer, when the heat has everyone on edge.

The big problem is that Dale Hinshaw doesn't have air-conditioning, which magnifies his irritability tenfold. He sits in his vinyl recliner wearing Bermuda shorts and a plaid cotton shirt, sweat coursing down his legs into his black dress socks and leather shoes. He reads the back issues of *The Mighty Men of God* newsletter and listens to talk radio. Cranky with heat and fueled with propaganda, he sets about enlisting the town in some great moral crusade.

The demonstration against Bob began at ten in the morning. Dale and his wife and Opal Majors were marching along with a noisy contingent from the Harmony Worship Center. A jet stream from the north had cooled things down. It was a comfortable eighty-two degrees with low humidity and a steady breeze. A perfect day for rabble-rousing. The marchers paraded back and forth in front of the *Herald* building carrying signs that read *Down with Bob!* and *Bob Must Go!*

At ten-thirty, they began chanting for Bob to come out, confess his sin, and get right with the Lord, but he wasn't in the building. He was sitting in the Legal Grounds across the street, with me, watching from the picture window that looked out onto Main Street.

"That Dale sure is a piece of work," Bob said.

"You oughta try being his pastor."

Bob shook his head. "These people remind me of my father. It isn't enough for them to have their views. They have to impose them on everyone else. I really don't even care for Bill Clinton. I just put that in there to make them mad."

"Looks like it worked."

Across the street, Dale had rolled a burn barrel from the back of a truck and was burning copies of the *Herald*.

"Is this a great country or what," Bob said. "I am free to print anything I want and Dale is free to burn it. Isn't that something!"

I agreed that it was marvelous.

"Though it is awful windy to be burning papers," Bob observed.

He'd no sooner said that, than a gust of wind picked up a burning section of newspaper, lifted it in the air, and carried it down the street, where it came to a smoldering stop underneath Dale's car, which had lately been leaking puddles of oil.

Unfortunately, Dale had worked himself into such a sanctimonious frenzy, he didn't notice the glow of fire spreading underneath his car.

"Do you suppose we ought to help him?" Bob asked.

"Probably we should."

Bob went behind the counter and lifted down a fire extinguisher hanging on the wall near the stove. He hurried through the front door and across the street to Dale's car, and began spraying the extinguisher in a futile effort to douse the flames, which had already reached the engine compartment and were accelerated by thirteen years of accumulated grease and oil. By the time the fire department arrived, Dale's car was engulfed. We stood watching as the tires exploded, one by one, and the gas tank ignited in a fiery ball.

Dale was cited for burning an open fire within town limits and holding a parade without a permit. The fire chief, Darrell Furbay, was thumbing through his code book, seeing whether he could charge Dale with any more infractions.

Bob Miles and I stood together, surveying the wreckage.

"I had no idea things would turn out like this," Bob said.

Though I didn't say so, I wasn't surprised. It was Dale's custom to leave ruination in his wake. What was unusual about this, and sweetly poetic, was that only Dale had born the brunt of his lunacy. Generally, when he went down, he dragged someone else with him.

Dale looked like a madman. His eyebrows were singed from where he'd tried to rescue his *Rapture—The Only Way to Fly!* license plate from the front bumper of his car.

"This is all your fault," he said to Bob Miles. "If you hadn't written those editorials, this'd never have happened. Don't think you can mock the Lord like this and get away with it." And with that, Dale turned and stalked off toward home, his long-suffering wife in tow, laden with signs.

To paraphrase Emerson, some people wear religion like an ill-fitting suit. And though some are improved by it, there seem to be just as many people made worse by it, folks who tried grace on and didn't like the way it fit.

I walked home thinking of all the money our church has given over the years to alleviate human suffering, though now I believe the world would have been better off if we'd used the money to buy Dale an air conditioner.

Eight

A Near Miss

*I*t took me sixteen days to learn pastors were expected to be perfect. I was fresh out of seminary and pastoring my first church, when I'd mentioned in a sermon that Barbara and I had fought that week. I said it in order to reveal my imperfections, to show the congregation I was one of them. It didn't work. The elders said if we didn't set a better example with our marriage, they'd find a minister who would.

So much for honesty, I thought. So much for sharing your struggles with the body of believers. So much for bearing one another's burdens and thus fulfilling the law of Christ.

After that, Barbara and I were careful to hold hands in public and gaze fondly at one another, even when we wanted to kill each other. Others in town could trade in their spouses the way some traded in cars, and people hardly blinked. But let me mention I'd gone to bed mad at my wife, and parents would cover their children's ears, lest they be tainted by the sacrilege.

In my twelfth year there, we had met with a marriage counselor in the next town who turned out to be related to an elder in our church. The counselor let it slip at a family reunion, and the next week I was hauled before the Sanhedrin, where I was ordered not to discuss my personal problems with other people. In fact, I was not supposed to have problems in the first place. And if I did, why couldn't I just go to the Lord in prayer? Could it be I no longer believed in the power of prayer? the elders wanted to know. They saw no alternative but to fire me, so they could hire a minister who took seriously Christ's command to be perfect.

Our biggest problem turned out to be that particular church. Once we moved, our marriage was fine. Now we get along well, so long as I don't work too many hours or volunteer my wife for tasks in the church, both of which I am prone to do.

To their credit, the people of Harmony Friends are more realistic when it comes to marriage, and though divorce is rare, so is passion. If I were to conduct a marriage enrichment program, no one would attend. When the pastor before me, Pastor Taylor, had preached a sermon on active listening in which he and his wife role-played effective communication in the Christian marriage, the offering for that week went down 60 percent. The next week he'd preached on sex for the Christian couple and was very nearly fired.

Occasionally, some of the church members will come to my office to unburden themselves and tell me the deepest secrets of their marriages, which, being nosy, I find a bit thrilling. Sometimes, though, I hear things I'd rather not think about, particularly about people's sex lives, or lack thereof. I've known these people most of my life and prefer to remain ignorant of certain aspects of their lives, the sex aspect being one of them.

Though nothing surprises me anymore, I was a bit taken aback when I came to my office early one August morning to find Dolores Hinshaw awaiting my arrival. She was visibly distraught; a handkerchief was knotted in her hands, and her eyes were red and swollen.

I pulled up a chair, sat beside her, and rested a hand on her arm. "What is it, Dolores?"

She opened her mouth to speak, but no words would come. She dabbed her eyes, blew her nose with a liquidy snort, and then blurted out, "It's Dale."

"Is something wrong with Dale?" It was a question whose answer was so obvious it scarcely required a response.

"I don't know how much more of it I can take," she said.

"More of what, Dolores? What happened?"

For the next hour, she poured out her soul, unloading forty-one years of resentment. Not only had he burned their car, he'd taken a thousand dollars she'd saved for their fiftieth anniversary cruise and given it to the Mighty Men of God ministry. "When I asked him not to, he told me the man is the head of household. If I hear him say that one more time, I might just choke him."

She felt guilty as soon as she said it, as if voicing her displeasure was somehow unfaithful. But after forty-one years of submission, she'd reached her limit.

As it turns out, the Mighty Men of God had mailed Dale a letter claiming to be under attack by liberal forces and needing Dale's "prayerful and tangible assistance" to beat back Satan's latest assault. Dale had written back, including a check for a thousand dollars. Just the week before, another burner on their stove had gone out. They were now down to one burner. It would cost a hundred dollars to fix the stove, which Dale had refused to pay. A thousand dollars to beat back the liberal tide they could afford, but not three new burners for their stove.

"I was so mad, I could have spit," she told me. "First the car, then the stove, and now our money's gone."

The month before, Miriam Hodge had given her a book written by an evangelical woman who had kicked off the traces and was challenging the Church to set its women free. Dolores had wrapped it in a plain brown wrapper and was reading it under the covers with a flashlight after Dale fell asleep. She had been thinking of taking the wrapper off and giving him a jolt.

But forty-one years of passivity was not easily overcome, so Dolores's rebellion had taken quieter forms. Dale hates wasting food, so she had begun adding large amounts of salt to his food, just for the pleasure of watching him choke it down with water, which she had also salted. When he complained about the food, she blamed it on the stove. "I must have got confused trying to cook three dishes on one burner. I'll try not to let it happen again," she said, as she spooned another portion onto his plate.

She wasn't proud of this, she told me, but felt she had no recourse.

Then she invited the town's most notorious liberals, Mabel and Deena Morrison, to their home for dinner. She didn't salt their food, but loaded down Dale's pretty good. When he complained, Mabel and Deena said it was probably his imagination, that their food tasted fine.

Mabel studied him closely. "Maybe you have this disease I was reading about the other day. Everything tastes salty and you're always thirsty. Next thing you know, you're worried all the time and your gums bleed when you brush your teeth and then you're dead, just like that," she said, with a snap of her fingers. "It's one of those diseases you get from mosquitoes."

The thing was, Dale had been noticing blood on his toothbrush lately.

"Have you been worried?" Mabel persisted.

"There's a godless, liberal assault against Bible-believing Americans," he'd said. "How could I not be worried?"

And two of them were right there at his dinner table. Deena Morrison was the worst of all. She was wearing a toe ring, which Dolores admired out loud, knowing it would irritate Dale, who believed toe rings were a sign of immorality.

"I went out and bought one just to make him mad," Dolores confided.

He had hit the roof. He was certain there was a verse against toe rings in the Bible, but after an exhaustive search couldn't find it. "If it's not against the Scriptures, it should be," he'd told her, and had ordered her to take it off; she was a mother, not a dance hall girl, he'd said.

The next day was trash day. She'd upped the ante by cutting slits in the trash bags, so the bottom would give out halfway down the driveway when Dale was carrying the trash to the curb. She'd watched from the kitchen window as the coffee grounds had trailed behind him like a snake. A soup can fell out about a quarter of the way down, which was when it first occurred to Dale he might have a problem. He'd picked up the pace and tried to make it to the curb before the bag split open.

It took Dolores three bags to get it right. If the slit was too small, Dale could make it to the curb without a hitch. If it was too big, he'd notice and use the wheelbarrow. Three inches turned out to be the optimum slit.

Thinking the bags were defective, he'd returned them to the Kroger for a refund and bought a new box. Dolores had lain low for a week to lull him into complacency, then struck with a vengeance—a three-inch slit with a rock in the bottom and spoiled chicken livers mixed with rotten eggs.

She confessed she had been thinking of leaving him, of moving to the city and living with her sister, but couldn't bring herself to walk away from forty-one years of marriage. Instead, she had tried not talking with him, which hadn't worked. "I could set myself on fire and he wouldn't notice," she told me. "All he does is ramble on about the church and liberals. He doesn't even ask me what I think. Last month it was Bob Miles and the *Herald*. This month it's the ushers."

There are two aisles at the Harmony meetinghouse. For years we've run an usher up each aisle, which requires only two ushers a week, so the rest of the ushers don't get much playing time. There had been some mumbling among the bench warmers, who wanted to switch to a zone collection, two men up each aisle with a floating usher in case of an injury. Five ushers a week, instead of two. It was a big change, something not to be taken lightly, so Dale had been holding regular meetings to pray about it.

"Then he comes home and turns on the TV and watches those kooks on Channel 41," she said. The "kooks" are the Reverend Rod Duvall and his pink-haired wife, who are prone to fits of crying, especially when they're asking for money, which is every other day. "I can't even sleep for listening to those two caterwauling."

I knew I was supposed to urge her to forgive Dale and be reconciled with him, but by then I was so worked up, I wanted to choke him myself.

Instead, I put my hand on her arm and prayed for her and for Dale and their marriage, then gave her a box of Kleenex to take with her. I suspected she'd need it.

At three o'clock the next morning, my telephone rang. It was Dolores, calling from the hospital in Cartersburg. She was hysterical. "It's Dale," she cried. "I think I've killed him."

He'd awakened several hours before, his head reeling, unable to walk for the room spinning. He'd crawled into the bathroom and vomited. She'd taken one look at him and ran to the phone to call Johnny Mackey to come with his ambulance. It took Johnny forty-five minutes to get there. He wasn't feeling all that well himself. But they finally made it to the hospital in Cartersburg, where they took Dale's blood pressure, then took it again just to be sure.

"It's a wonder you haven't exploded," the doctor told Dale. "Do you put a lot of salt in your food?"

"No, lately it's been salty enough," Dale said.

Dolores paled.

"That's probably why you're dizzy. You're retaining water, and it's messed up your inner ears and your equilibrium. Salt will do that every time. I'm putting you on a low-sodium diet." The doctor shook his head as he wrote. "It's a wonder you didn't have a stroke and die."

That was when she'd phoned me.

Dale's blood pressure was so high, they kept him in the hospital overnight. I drove over the next morning to visit him. Dolores was seated in a chair next to his bed, stroking his hair.

I visited for a while, then said a prayer for Dale. I thanked God for sparing his life, then went from prayer to editorializing, pondering aloud whether our brushes with death might be the Lord's way of causing us to reflect on certain things, like how we treat our spouses, for instance.

Then I said "Amen" and promised Dale I would visit him the next day. Dolores followed me out of the room.

"You won't tell him what I did, will you?" she asked, when we were out of earshot of Dale.

"I won't tell a soul," I promised. "But maybe you and Dale should get some marriage counseling."

"He'd never do it. He doesn't believe in it. Besides, he'd never listen. He doesn't listen to anyone."

I gave her a hug. "You come see me whenever you need to blow off a little steam. It's probably better than salting him to death."

I walked out of the hospital, thinking back on the first years of my marriage. Sometimes I marvel that we've made it. When Dolores had mentioned how Dale never listened, I tried not to think of all the evenings I'd spent in my recliner, responding to my wife with monosyllabic grunts.

To be heard, to have someone who will listen, might be our deepest human need. I marvel that Dolores had gone forty-one years without it.

I didn't go to the office. I went home instead. My wife was upstairs, folding laundry on our bed. I asked her where the boys were. Over at the Grants' house playing, she said. She asked what I was doing home. I told her I missed her. She smiled, and then she talked, and as she spoke I listened, lying on my back, my feet propped on the footboard.

Then we did something else, which I won't talk about, preferring to keep that aspect of our lives a private matter.

"What's that on your foot?" I asked afterward.

"A toe ring," she said. "How do you like it?"

"I like it very much, though don't you think it's a bit racy for a minister's wife?"

"It depends on the minister's wife," she said. "I say if you've got the toes for it, then why not."

Why not, indeed.

n i n e

Love and Rumors of Love

$\mathcal{T}$he heat had continued through much of July and into August, but was broken the second week of August by a thunderstorm that ushered in a cool breeze from the north, carrying with it the scent of pine trees and lakes. All over town, people turned off their air conditioners and opened their windows.

It's been a quiet month. Attendance is down at the churches and several of the businesses have closed while their owners are on vacation. Ned Kivett has taken his annual fishing trip to Minnesota, leaving his cashier, Nora Nagle, to run the Five and Dime. Kyle Weathers locked the barbershop and posted a sign on the door announcing he would return in two weeks. He didn't tell anyone where he was going, fueling speculation he was up to no good.

I was at the Coffee Cup on a Tuesday morning, where the conversation turned to Kyle and what sin he was likely pursuing and with whom. The consensus of the Coffee Cup crowd is that he has driven to Florida to visit a woman he met on the Internet. Kyle is one of those men who are defeated by proximity. Distance is his ally.

Women who've never met him, except over the Internet, find him witty and urbane. If he were to leave it at that, he would have no shortage of female admirers. Unfortunately, they eventually meet in person, causing Kyle to suffer the pain of rejection time and again.

He had been spending his mornings at the Five and Dime admiring Nora Nagle, hoping to strike up a romance with her. Though she would enjoy the companionship of a man, she is not so desperate that Kyle would be seen as a viable choice. He has a great wing of hair on the left side of his head, which he combs over to cover his balding crown. That she could overlook, were it not for the profusion of hair growing in thick tufts from his nose and ears.

Doctor Neely has also left town for his first vacation in twenty years. He and his wife, Marcella, have taken a two-week trip to France. It was a gift from their daughters, who knew their parents would never leave town unless forced to do so. People were not at all pleased with this abdication of responsibility, and several of them considered getting sick and dying just to teach him a lesson.

Fern Hampton has had a mole on her left knee for over fifty years, but about five years ago it began changing shapes. It used to look like Rhode Island, but was now the shape of Ohio and starting to resemble Texas. She was convinced it was cancerous and had been meaning to consult Dr. Neely for the past several years. When she read in the *Herald* that he had flitted off to Europe, she phoned his answering service, demanding he catch the next plane home.

Instead, she was informed Dr. Neely's patients would be attended by a Dr. Daniel Pierce, who would be happy to look at Fern's knee. This upset her even further. What made them think she'd be willing to bare her naked knee to a total stranger? She fumed about it to anyone who'd listen, warning the Friendly Women's Circle that a pervert with a knee fetish had come to town, jeopardizing their chastity. This tripled his business, as unattached ladies all over town made appointments, hoping to become the object of his passion.

Deena Morrison went to visit him on a Wednesday afternoon, during the slow hours at the Legal Grounds. Her upper legs had been itching for several weeks. She'd put off going to the doctor, he being male and she being modest. But finally she couldn't bear it and phoned on Wednesday morning for an appointment that afternoon.

She sat in the waiting room for close to an hour, watching a parade of women file into his office and walk out ten minutes later, starry-eyed.

Hester Gladden was seated beside her. "Have you met Dr. Pierce yet?" she asked Deena.

"No. This is my first visit. I have a rash on my legs."

"This is my fourth time to see him," Hester confided.

"Oh, have you been sick?"

"Never felt better," Hester said. She sighed. "Sure wish I was thirty years younger, though."

Finally, the nurse called Deena's name and escorted her to an examination room, where she was measured (five feet, four inches), weighed (a hundred and eighteen pounds), asked to remove her clothes, and handed a paper gown. Now she was remembering why she seldom visited the doctor.

She kept her clothes on and began studying the room. Diplomas hung on the wall, a glass jar with Q-tips sat next to the sink, an eye chart was fixed to the back of the door. A skeleton Dr. Neely had purchased at a medical auction years before and loaned to the Rotary Club each Halloween for its haunted house stood in the corner, ogling her, its teeth fixed in a permanent leer. She draped the paper gown over it, then sat on the stool and began thumbing through a pamphlet on diseases of the liver.

She heard the doctor before she saw him. "Haroldeena Morrison," he said, apparently reading from her chart. "That poor woman, they really hung it on her."

Although she had never cared for her full name and preferred Deena, it rankled her that a total stranger would comment on it.

The door swung open, and in stepped Dr. Pierce.

"I've had that name twenty-nine years and it's worked just fine," Deena snapped, rather uncharacteristically. "I'll thank you to keep your opinion to yourself." And without even a glance in his direction, she stalked from the room and out the front door.

By Friday afternoon, her skin was raw from scratching. The rash had spread to both legs and up onto her stomach. She decided to close early and go home for an oatmeal bath. She was putting away the coffee pots when the bell over the door tinkled. She looked up as a handsome young man with blond hair, blue eyes, and a cleft in his chin walked into the Legal Grounds.

"Excuse me," he said. "I'm looking for a Miss Deena Morrison."

This was just the way she'd always dreamed it would happen—a ruggedly handsome man would walk into her coffee shop, seeking her out.

"I'm Deena."

"I'm Dr. Pierce," he said. "And I've come to apologize for my rudeness the other day. I don't know what I was thinking. I hope you'll forgive me."

She looked at the slight cleft in his chin and his strong jawbone and suddenly felt quite charitable. "Apology accepted." She extended her hand and he shook it. As hands go, his was a nice one, with neatly clipped nails, his handshake firm but sensitive.

"How are you feeling?" he asked.

"Fine," she said. "And you?"

"I'm doing well, thank you. I didn't get to examine you Wednesday. Are you feeling better today?"

"Not really," she said. "I have a rash and it's spreading."

"Where is it exactly?"

"Umm, well, it started on my upper legs and now it's moved to my stomach."

"Would you like me to look at it as long as I'm here?"

She glanced out the front windows. "It's not very private here. Maybe I should just call your office and reschedule."

"I'm leaving town for the weekend," Dr. Pierce said. "I couldn't see you until next Tuesday. I'd feel better if I could just look at it now. Do you have a back room?"

"Well, there's the supply room," Deena said.

"I can examine you there," he offered. "Really, it's the least I can do."

"Yes, I suppose that would be fine."

She led him to the supply room, flipped on the light, and pulled up her shirt a half inch to expose her midriff.

"When did this start?" he asked.

"A couple of weeks ago"

"And you say it started in your groin region."

She blushed. "Yes, that's right."

"Could you ease your shirt up a notch higher. I can't quite make this out."

She turned her head away and lifted her shirt another inch.

"Hmm," he said. "Very interesting."

I wonder now why they didn't hear the bell over the door tinkle when I entered the Legal Grounds looking for my wife, who occasionally helped at the coffee shop. I heard voices in the storage room, so I walked behind the counter and looked in, just in time to see Dr. Pierce, whom I'd met earlier that day at the Rexall drugstore, studying Deena's midsection with great interest.

I barely had time to apologize for intruding on their private moment, before Deena pulled down her shirt and ran past me and out the door, her face beet red.

"Ringworm," Doctor Pierce said, straightening up. "Most unpleasant, but curable."

"It sounds gross," I said. "Worms, yuck."

"Actually, they're not worms. It's a fungus." He looked around the storage room. "Where'd she go?"

"Out."

"Does she have a history of bolting from rooms?" he asked.

"Not to my knowledge."

"She strikes me as an impetuous woman."

"She's really quite nice," I said.

"Well, now she has ringworm. She'll need medicine. I have some samples back at the office. Could you tell me where she lives?"

Since both his office and Deena's house were on my way home, I volunteered to take the medicine to her. I had to knock five times before she would come to the door.

I handed her the medicine, told her she had ringworm, and repeated what Dr. Pierce told me. "Apply it three times a day, wipe down your shower with bleach, and don't share a towel with anyone. It's highly contagious."

"What did he say about me?" she asked.

"I think he finds you interesting."

"Thank you for the medicine, Sam."

"That's okay. I'm sorry if I startled you. I didn't mean to embarrass you."

"That's all right. I shouldn't be so jumpy."

"Is everything all right, Deena?"

She sighed. "I'm twenty-nine years old, don't have a prospect in the world, and the most handsome man in town thinks I'm crazy. And I've just been told I have worms. Other than that, everything's fine."

"Actually, it's just a fungus."

"Oh, that's much better. I'm sure he thinks I'm the picture of feminine charm. Fungi are much more attractive than worms."

She thanked me for bringing the medicine. I left for home, but then remembered I hadn't finished my sermon, so I headed back to my office instead. Frank was there, putting the final touches on Sunday's bulletin. I phoned my wife to tell her I would be home a little late, and mentioned Deena's ringworm to her.

The next day we worked in the yard, mowing, trimming, and pulling weeds. It was a beautiful Saturday, and the clouds were puffy and white as sheets. That evening, we went to the fire-department fish fry, then came home and sat on the porch while the boys caught fireflies, pinching their lights off to make rings.

I arrived at church the next morning an hour early and set out the bulletins on the table near the door, surveying the list of persons in need of prayer. It had grown to fifty-three names, many of whom were now fully recovered but enjoyed being prayed for and insisted their names remain. At the bottom of the list was Deena Morrison's name, followed by the word *ringworm*.

Frank came in the door as I was reading the bulletin.

"Morning, Frank. I see Deena called to be put on the prayer list."

"Nope. I heard you tell your wife she had ringworm and thought I'd add her name."

"I wish you hadn't done that," I said. "I think Deena wanted it kept a secret."

"Then why'd you tell your wife?" Frank asked.

"I tell my wife a lot of things that are meant to be private."

"So you admit to being a gossip, then."

I gathered up the offending bulletins. "Maybe we'll just do without a bulletin today."

"Can't do that. The words to the last hymn are on the back cover. Why don't I just go through and black out Deena's name with a pen?"

"Do you mind?"

"No, I suppose not." He let out a heavy, inconvenienced sigh.

Halfway through the opening minute of meditation, it occurred to me we'd have been better off throwing the bulletins away and picking a new closing hymn. Half the congregation were holding their bulletins up to the lights trying to make out what Frank had crossed out.

"The first letter's a *D*," Ellis Hodge whispered to Miriam. "It's probably Dale."

"It can't be," Hester Gladden piped up behind them. "The second name starts with an *M*."

Ellis glanced around the meeting room, eyeing each person, looking for a fit to the initials DM. His glance settled on Deena Morrison. Slowly, others in the meeting room stole glances at her, trying to discern her medical condition.

"I can't be sure," Dale Hinshaw called out, "but I think it says *ringworm*."

Hester Gladden turned toward Deena. "I thought you went to the doctor."

"Who went to the doctor?" Opal Majors asked, while reaching into her ear to adjust her hearing aid.

"Deena Morrison," Fern Hampton said.

"What's wrong with Deena?" Opal asked.

"Dale said she has the worms," Hester said.

With that, Deena stood, mustering all the dignity she could, and strode from the meetinghouse.

The next day she hung a *Closed for Vacation* sign on the door of the Legal Grounds and hasn't been seen for a week. The rumor circulating in the booths at the Coffee Cup is that she has run off to Florida to elope with Kyle Weathers, though I know for a fact it isn't true. If I were a gossip, I could set the rumor straight, but since I don't indulge in such practices, I can't mention how I saw her in Cartersburg in the company of a handsome young man with a cleft in his chin, looking positively radiant, albeit a tad itchy.

Ten

It Takes a Thief

The thunderstorm that hit in mid-August was all boom and very little rain, and by the last week of August the ground was parched, six inches of rain below normal. The farmers have been gathering each morning at the Coffee Cup to lament their predicament and hinting that if I had any pull with the Lord, I would deliver a good, steady rain on their behalf.

Farmers, I have discovered, are a generally gloomy lot, and when not worrying about the weather are direly predicting equipment failures or falling crop prices. If my prayers did produce rain, they would grumble that it didn't come in quarter-inch increments, equally disbursed over the growing season. My role in this is abundantly clear—I am to curry the favor of the rain god, lest their livelihoods be ruined and my suitability for ministry questioned.

By the last week of August, the drought was so bad, Harvey Muldock and the other men of the town council imposed a ban on lawn and garden watering. In an article in the *Herald,* Harvey was quoted as saying the town's water department would be monitoring each home's water use and prosecuting scofflaws. The men at the American Legion detected a whiff of fascism and issued a proclamation declaring their opposition to the council's latest tyranny.

The town-council elections are in November, and it was Harvey's hope, when he proposed the watering ban, that it would make someone mad enough to run against him and he could retire from the town council altogether. He's served for sixteen years. He ran for the office to prove to his wife he could win, after he'd mentioned in passing that he'd been thinking of running and she'd laughed and told him to stop being ridiculous. So just to prove he could, he ran and won. Now she won't let him quit. The council meets every Monday night, which gets him out of the house so she can have her euchre club over. The last thing she wants is Harvey hanging around trying to be witty and charming, making a pest of himself.

It took several years for Harvey to realize he'd been duped into running. Now his only hope is to irritate enough people to be voted out of office. He is tired of the grind, weary of people phoning his home at all hours to complain about things over which he has no control. The last straw was when Hester Gladden phoned his house during his favorite TV program to complain that a groundhog was tearing up her garden and wanting to know what he was going to do about it.

The next evening, after dark, he took his .22 rifle down from the closet shelf and walked over to Hester's house to dispatch the groundhog, though it occurred to him it would be infinitely more satisfying to take out Hester. He was hiding behind her tulip tree when he noticed Hester sneak out of her house and drag her garden hose over to Bea Majors's water spigot next door. He watched as Hester hooked up her hose to Bea's spigot and adjusted the sprinkler to water her grass.

He tiptoed to Bea's door and rang her doorbell until lights flickered on throughout the house as she awakened. He didn't stick around to watch the clash, but noticed the next morning at church that Bea and Hester weren't speaking to one another.

Hester has been the Friendly Women Circle's treasurer nearly twenty years. At their next meeting, without revealing the sordid details of the water heist, Bea suggested it might be wise to audit their books. "There are things you don't know that I'm not at liberty to discuss," she said. "But it might behoove us to examine our books and appoint a new treasurer."

Miriam Hodge pointed out there had never been more than a hundred dollars in the Friendly Women Circle's checking account, and that checks required two signatures.

"She's been putting her trash in my garbage can for years," Bea sputtered angrily. "Now she's stealing my water." Bea turned to Hester. "You didn't think I'd noticed, did you? And to think I invited you to join this honorable body. What was I thinking?"

The women gasped, and shifted away from Hester. To have one of their own exposed as a common thief was more than they could bear. If word ever got out, their stock would plummet; they'd be ruined.

"As much as it hurts me to say this," Fern Hampton said to Hester, "I'm afraid we'll have to ask you to resign."

It actually didn't hurt a bit. Fern hasn't liked Hester Gladden since 1989, when Hester had the temerity to run against her for the

Circle's presidency. According to Fern, Hester's defeat was one more indication of the Lord's protective hedge around the Circle.

"Aren't we moving awfully fast?" Miriam Hodge asked. "We haven't even heard Hester's side of it. And even if it's true, aren't we supposed to forgive?"

Although the Friendly Women's Circle is strong on noodles and fairly adept at organization, forgiveness has never been their strong suit. Three minutes later, Hester was ousted as treasurer and Jessie Peacock was being sworn in, her left hand resting on a 1935 first-edition copy of the Friendly Women's cookbook, her right hand upraised, as she pledged to defend the Friendly Women's Circle from all enemies, foreign and domestic. Then they brought the meeting to a quick close, so they could go home and begin circulating word of Hester's fall from grace.

Harvey was working at the dealership, and didn't learn of Hester's overthrow until that night at the supper table, when Eunice spilled the beans, describing in great detail Hester's transgressions and her eviction from the treasurer's position.

Brilliant, Harvey thought. Why didn't I think of that? I'll steal something, and they'll have to throw me off the council.

He started the next day, visiting the town hall during his lunch break and pocketing a box of paper clips in plain view of Dottie, the billing clerk.

"You need some paper clips, Harvey?" Dottie asked. "Help yourself. Somebody works as hard as you do for this town ought to get a box of paper clips every now and then."

"I'm gonna take a stapler too," he said. "Mine's broken."

"Funny you should mention that," she said, reaching into her desk drawer. "I brought an extra one from home just yesterday. You take it for as long as you need it."

This wasn't going at all as he'd planned. If Dottie didn't start cooperating, he'd never be a thief. He glanced around the office. His eyes fell on the soda pop machine. He ambled across the room, reached behind the machine where Dottie hid the key, unlocked the machine door, pulled out a Nehi orange pop, and took a swig.

"Let me buy that for you," Dottie said, fishing through her purse for change. "I owe you one from last week. Remember?"

Harvey sighed. That was the problem with people nowadays, he thought. They're too soft on crime. Whatever happened to the good old days when they hanged criminals?

On the way home, he walked past the *Herald* building just as Owen Stout was depositing a quarter in the newspaper dispenser. As Owen opened the door to get the paper, Harvey leaned in beside him. "Don't shut it yet," he said, reaching past Owen to grab a copy of the paper from the dispenser.

Bob Miles was working on his "Bobservation Post" column, reporting the Tuesday afternoon view from the front window of the *Herald*, and saw the whole thing. He was aghast. Larceny on his doorstep! By a public servant, no less!

When the newspaper hit the doorsteps two days later, the first line of the "Bobservation Post" read, "What member of the town council was recently seen STEALING a newspaper?" Bob's article went on to lament the decline of integrity among politicians, starting with Watergate and winding its way through the Iran-Contra scandal, Bill

Clinton's impeachment, and now a brazen theft in broad daylight by a town councilman.

What kind of example did this set for the children in town? Bob wanted to know.

There are three members on the town council—Harvey, Owen Stout, and Clevis Nagle. Clevis was out of town that week with his wife on their annual trip to visit her brother in Des Moines, so he was ruled out, which left Harvey and Owen. Owen is an attorney, and an honest one, but because people like to believe the worst about lawyers, they assumed he was the culprit and letters to the editor began rolling in demanding his ouster from the council.

Owen was going to let it pass, but his wife wouldn't and wrote a letter to the *Herald* defending her husband. Unfortunately, by insisting on Owen's innocence, she inadvertently implicated Harvey. This annoyed people to no end. In all their lives, they had never seen such a malicious and blatant political attack. Harvey couldn't go anywhere without people stopping him to voice their support.

Harvey refrained from any public comment, which was seen as yet another example of his sterling character. People began sending him money for his reelection campaign. The Odd Fellows convened a special meeting, a first in their long and noble history, and named Harvey the recipient of their first annual Civic Leader of the Year Award.

Harvey began to panic. At this rate, the townspeople would not only vote Owen off the council, they'd carry Harvey through town on their shoulders and install him as council president for life. He thought of publicly confessing, but was growing accustomed to the adulation and even starting to enjoy its privileges. The day before, he'd eaten at the Coffee Cup and Ned Kivett had insisted on buying his lunch. Vinny Toricelli had mowed his yard, and his name had been added to the prayer lists at all the churches so everyone would remember to pray for him and Eunice as they came under Satanic attack.

Judy Iverson wrote a letter to the *Herald* pointing out Harvey had served for sixteen years without a dime of compensation and suggested it was time for a tax hike so council members could be paid.

It was about this time that the idea of being president for life began appealing to Harvey.

Unfortunately, the only one able to set the record straight was Bob Miles, who was faced with having to chose between journalistic integrity and money. It did not take Bob long to decide. Harvey was Bob's largest advertiser—a twenty-dollar back-page ad every week for his car dealership. Though Bob felt sorry for Owen, Owen hadn't advertised in the paper for years.

Bob toyed with the idea of blackmailing Harvey. But, then, *blackmail* was such a harsh word. Actually, he thought of it as *laissez-faire* capitalism, which he explained to Harvey when he came in the *Herald* office to pay his advertising bill.

Bob was seated at his desk by the front window.

"Quite a view you got there," Harvey commented as he laid a twenty on Bob's desk for that week's ad.

"It sure is," Bob said. "I can see everything on the town square from here. Anybody does anything, and I can see it."

"Everything?" Harvey asked.

"Yep. Everything."

"So how's business?" Harvey asked, changing the subject.

"Been pretty good. Got a phone call the other day from someone wanting to buy the entire back page for the next year."

"The back page?" Harvey said. "But that's my page. You've always put me on the back page."

"Well, they've offered me fifty dollars for it. But don't worry, we can always run your ad on the classifieds page."

"The classifieds page!" Harvey was indignant. "No one ever reads the classifieds. You can't do that to me."

"Nothin' personal, Harvey. Just business. Course if you wanted to buy the back page, I could let you have it for the same price as the other fella." Then Bob leaned back in his chair. "Yes, this sure is some view I have here."

Well, what was Harvey to do? What is a man to do when, despite his best efforts, he finds himself the most respected man in town and suddenly has a reputation to uphold? He bought the entire back page for one year, though not cheerfully.

Harvey stopped by my house that evening seeking absolution for his sins. He told me the whole sordid story while sitting on my front porch.

"I don't feel bad about Hester," he said. "She got what she had comin'. But I wish Owen hadn't been dragged into it. I'm sorry about that."

"Maybe you should apologize to Owen."

"I don't feel *that* bad," he said.

"Well, what do you want from me, then?" I asked.

"Just wanted to get this off my chest, and it helped. I feel a whole lot better."

"Don't you think you'd feel even better if you confessed to stealing the newspaper?"

Harvey thought for a moment. "No, I don't think so." He paused. "So am I forgiven, Sam?"

"It's not up to me to forgive you, Harvey. You didn't wrong me. If you want forgiveness, you should go see Owen."

"You know, the Catholics, they can go to their priest and the priest'll have 'em say a few prayers and they're forgiven."

"Well, Harvey, we're not Catholic."

"Not yet anyway," Harvey grumbled. "But I'm giving it serious thought."

Harvey sat quietly for several minutes. "So what would people think of me if I told the truth?"

"I know I would respect you a great deal, and I imagine others would too."

"It's just that it's felt pretty nice with everybody treating me special. It's nice to be respected."

"It sure is," I agreed. "And the way you get respected is to be respectable."

"Yeah, I suppose so."

It began raining that night, just in time to save the corn, which gave people something else to talk about. The next day Harvey lifted the watering ban, and Hester's groundhog was struck dead by Amanda Hodge, who'd had her driver's permit less than thirty minutes before taking a life. It wasn't a very auspicious start, even though Hester seemed profoundly grateful.

That week Harvey ran his first full-page ad—a letter of confession with an apology to Owen Stout, which was graciously accepted. All in all, it was a good way to end the month—a farmers' rain, soft on the roof, a fitting repentance, and the death of a marauding groundhog.

Eleven

Labor Day

Labor Day has descended and people are finding their way back to church after their summer hiatus. Sunday school classes are resuming, with one exception. The Live Free or Die Sunday school class, founded by Robert Miles, Sr., in 1960 to guard against Communist infiltration in the meeting, has closed its doors. Dale Hinshaw had taught the class the past four years after Robert Miles, Sr., left in a huff to join the Baptist church. It's taken four years for people to realize that an hour with Dale Hinshaw is a bad way to start their week.

The class has been losing membership for several years, it being difficult to get folks worked up against the Soviet Union after it no longer existed. Dale had made a valiant effort to draw the class's attention to other threats, such as Democrats and Unitarians, but without much luck. He grew bitter about the congregation's lack of hostility. "For crying out loud, why even go to church, if you're not gonna fight the Lord's enemies?" It saddens Dale that people have lost their passion for true godliness.

With the official closing of the class, the four remaining members invaded Judy Iverson's young-adult class. Suddenly, the
prospect of teaching the children with Alice Stout didn't seem as
daunting and she asked if we could switch classes yet again. By
then, I had tired of flannelgraphs and trying to explain to the children that God hadn't really ordered the deaths of entire nations of
people. So back I went to the young adults and the remnants of the
Live Free or Die class.

Dale couldn't bring himself to sit under my instruction and
began attending the women's class, which meets in the basement
around the noodle table. On the first Sunday of the class, he read
aloud from Paul's First Letter to Timothy, that women should learn
in silence with all submissiveness, then tried to take over. But Fern
Hampton, a retired schoolteacher, was fortunate enough to have
taught back in the days when teachers knew how to apply pain to
various parts of the body to achieve a desired result. She gripped
the back of Dale's neck, causing him to go limp as a noodle. She
raised him from his seat, marched him up the basement steps, and
deposited him with a thud at the door of my classroom.

I use the word *classroom* loosely. When I had proposed we begin
a new Sunday school class for the young adults, I was met with stiff
resistance. Why, the argument went, we already had perfectly good
Sunday school classes, one for the men and one for the women.
Why couldn't the young adults attend those classes? What made
them so special that they needed their own class? That was the
problem with this generation, they wanted everything to revolve
around them. Besides, there was no place for them to meet.

But I persevered, and they finally relented when I agreed to clean the coatroom just inside the front door and hold the class there. Frank and I spent several hours that summer painting the room, making it presentable. This caused considerable ire among the remnants of the Live Free and Die class, who complained that they had never had a classroom of their own, and maybe if they had, their class would still be meeting.

The first day of Sunday school they shuffled into the coatroom, eyeing the young adults rather suspiciously. Stanley Farlow handed me a stack of dog-eared papers—the original typed pages of the Live Free or Die Sunday school curriculum, written by Robert J. Miles, Sr., himself in 1960.

"We teach from this," he said. "We're on lesson twelve, 'Better Dead Than Red.'"

"That's fine, Stanley, but we don't use a curriculum in this class," I said, handing it back. "This is a discussion group. Why don't you put this someplace where it'll be safe."

I welcomed everyone to the class, then shared the process I had in mind. Everybody in the class would be given small slips of paper on which they could anonymously write any theological question they wished us to consider. We'd put the slips in a hat and pull one out each Sunday to discuss, and perhaps together we could arrive at some insight or truth.

Stanley Farlow frowned. Truth by consensus was apparently not his preferred method of enlightenment. "Why don't you just tell us what the Bible says? Ain't that good enough anymore?"

"We'll certainly consult the Bible," I assured him. "But we also need to remember that Quakers believe truth can come from a variety of sources."

I expected Dale to object, but he was slumped in the corner, still dazed from his encounter with Fern.

The upside of the class was the presence of Deena Morrison and Dr. Pierce, who've been coming to church together for the past two weeks. It is an unparalleled joy to look up from my chair behind the pulpit and see the lovely Deena Morrison in the company of a handsome, young man. And a doctor, no less.

Deena introduced Dr. Pierce to the class, we exchanged greetings, and I began distributing slips of paper and pencils for people to write their questions.

"This is a splendid idea," Dr. Pierce said. "I've always wanted to participate in something like this."

One by one, people passed their questions around to me, which I deposited in my lawn-mowing hat I'd brought from home. "Now remember," I said, going over the rules once again, "we'll discuss only one question per week and we can't dodge a question just because we don't like it or it makes us uncomfortable."

"Agreed," everyone said, smiling enthusiastically.

In that moment, I had a vision of us engaged in serious reflection on the role of Scripture, the meaning of the Resurrection, and other topics that had plagued theologians for centuries.

I closed my eyes, reached my hand into the hat, stirred the papers around, then plucked one out. I studied the question before I read it. It was spidery, old-man writing.

"Read it out loud," Uly Grant said, urging me along.

"I can't quite make it out," I said. "Maybe I should pull out another question."

"Let me see it," my wife said, reaching over and taking it from my hand.

"What's it say?" Deena asked.

My wife studied the paper, then read, "Why can't we study lesson twelve?"

"I thought I'd already explained that," I said. "This class doesn't use a curriculum." I pulled another question from the hat and prepared to read it.

"I thought we was only gonna have one question a Sunday," Stanley Farlow said.

"That was the intention," I said. "But this is a little different."

"Well, that's a fine how-do-you-do," he said. "This class is only ten minutes old and we've already caught you lyin'."

Catching the scent of a crippled teacher, Dale had revived and was moving in for the kill. "I think that pretty well shows us what we have to look forward to. I say we need a new teacher, somebody we can trust to tell the truth. I'd like to volunteer my services."

"Sounds good to me," Stanley Farlow said. Stanley Farlow had not uttered a half dozen words in my presence in the four years I'd pastored Harmony Friends, but now he wouldn't shut up.

The young adults paled. My mind raced, trying to think of a way to avert this catastrophe. I glanced around the room, seeking an ally in my looming struggle against Dale and his minions.

Dr. Pierce was the first to speak. "Mr. Hinshaw, I'd be all for you teaching the class, were it not against the Bible."

"What do you mean, against the Bible?" Dale asked.

"Second Titus, third chapter, ninth verse," Dr. Pierce said. "As all are not called to be pastors, so shall ye let them instruct the believers and not obstruct them."

This seemed to give Dale pause. "I never heard that one before, but I sure don't wanna go against the Word."

Although I knew the Apostle Paul had written one letter to Titus, I was unaware he had written a second one, but wasn't about to say so, since Dale appeared to be wavering.

I took advantage of his uncertainty and reached into my lawn-mowing hat to pull out a second question, which I read aloud to the class. "Why do some Christians oppose abortion but support capital punishment?"

It was a question I had pondered many times over the years, but had never asked aloud for fear of losing my job.

The men of the Live Free or Die class, who were generally fond of capital punishment, frowned.

"I'll tell you why," Mabel Morrison said. "Because they don't know their keesters from a hole in the ground, that's why."

There was nothing like having a liberal in the class to get the ball rolling.

A spirited discussion followed, with Dale and Mabel circling one another like two bulldogs, growling and nipping at one another. At first, I tried to mediate, but it soon became clear Dale and Mabel weren't interested in finding common ground. By the end of the hour, my stomach was in knots and I wanted to vomit.

Dr. Pierce shook my hand after class. "That certainly was bracing," he said. "I had no idea when I wrote that question it would create such a lively debate."

Dale didn't stay for worship. He gathered up Dolores and left the meetinghouse in a huff.

The fertilizer hit the fan the next day, when Miriam Hodge stopped by my house to tell me she'd received a half dozen phone calls about the new class. "It was Dale and the men from his old Sunday school class," she said. "They want the class shut down."

"This isn't even their class," I pointed out. They just showed up and tried to take over."

Miriam sighed. "I know that, but they're really mad. Dale said Mabel Morrison called him a knucklehead and Dr. Pierce lied to him about a passage of Scripture. He wants them to apologize in front of the entire church next Sunday."

"That will never happen, and if we insist on it, we'll probably lose her and Deena and Dr. Pierce and half the young adults in my class."

"Dale said he's not coming back unless they agree to apologize."

My heart leaped at the thought. "Are you serious? He said that? That he wouldn't be back until they apologize? That's wonderful. Let's quit while we're ahead."

"It's not that simple, Sam. Dale phoned Fern and told her. She's demanded a special meeting of the Christian Education Committee be held this Friday. She thinks the class ought to be canceled, that it's too divisive."

"This is crazy. Fern's the one who sent him to my class. Did he mention that he tried to take it over? He's the one who should apologize."

"Folks are very upset, Sam. They don't understand why the young adults just can't attend the regular Sunday school classes."

"Not everyone wants to be in a traditional Sunday school class. We have a dozen new people coming to Sunday school who've never attended before. If we tell them they have to go to Fern or Dale's class, they'll stop coming altogether."

Just then a thought occurred to me, one so wicked I could barely voice it. "You don't suppose Fern and Dale did this on purpose, do you? They've been against this class from the start."

"Miriam thought for a moment. "I don't think so. I try never to attribute to malice anything that can be adequately explained by stupidity."

I chuckled. "Yes, you're probably right. But what do you think we should do?"

"You keep on teaching your class and let me handle the fallout. That's my job after all."

"Thank you, Miriam. I appreciate your support."

She shook her head. "I don't know why anyone would ever want to be a minister with people like Dale in the church."

"Because there are also people like you in the church."

She smiled.

"Thanks for stopping by, Miriam," I said, giving her a hug.

The called meeting of the Christian Education Committee never materialized. It seems Miriam and Ellis Hodge decided to throw a last-minute cookout on Friday night and invite the entire church. Apparently, eating Miriam's food was a far more pleasant prospect than sitting in the church basement with Fern Hampton, and no one showed up for the meeting except Fern.

It was a lovely late summer evening at the Hodge farm. Amanda took the children for hayrides while the young adults mingled with the old-timers, laughing and eating and telling stories. Dolores Hinshaw came, but Dale stayed away, which was sad, though also a relief. Dr. Pierce and Deena were present, holding hands, which people tried not to stare at, though everyone did. And when they shared the same fork to eat dessert, we knew it was true love.

After supper, Ellis strung a volleyball net between two trees, and we divided into teams and played into the evening hours. I was the line judge, seated under the oak tree, watching the ball loft back and forth across the net, occasionally thinking of Dale and Fern off by themselves, stewing, while life went merrily on, oblivious to their indignation.

Twelve

Scandal

*F*or the first time in memory, the Friendly Women's Circle Chicken Noodle Dinner has been postponed, causing much wailing and gnashing of teeth among the ladies of the church. They were ready to roll the second Sunday of September—the noodle freezer was full to overflowing, the pies and cakes were baked, the Tastee bread purchased, the plates stacked next to the silverware, and the tablecloths (embroidered in 1967 by the late Juanita Harmon before her grisly expiration in a stove explosion) stretched across the folding tables in the meetinghouse basement. I had even prayed over the noodles, asking the Lord to bless them to the nourishment of our bodies, that we might be strengthened to do His good work while there was yet time.

Then, on the Thursday before the dinner, Clevis Nagle from the Odd Fellows Lodge phoned the meetinghouse to inform us the Corn and Sausage Days parade had been temporarily delayed, on account of Harvey Muldock's 1951 Plymouth Cranbrook convertible giving up the ghost.

Why the parade and the dinner hinged on the well-being of Harvey's convertible is a mystery I've yet to fathom, but some questions are best left unasked, so I've kept out of it. Three weeks earlier, Harvey had stood during Joys and Concerns to ask for prayer for his beloved Cranbrook, so I knew something was wrong. Unfortunately, Harvey was in no condition to elaborate, as the merest mention of his car caused his eyes to swell with tears and his chin to tremble.

His melodramatics haven't sat well with Eunice, his wife. This past summer she'd undergone a hysterectomy, which Harvey had sailed through unfazed. He'd joked about her taking a Medicare vacation and wanted to know when she'd be back to cooking and doing the laundry. She'd asked him to mention it at church, so people would know, but he'd forgotten. But let his car not start, and he'd hammer the gates of heaven.

He'd gone out to start the Cranbrook in late August to ready it for the parade and found it wouldn't start. At first, he wasn't too concerned. He'd charged the battery, cleaned the points and plugs, and cleaned the carburetor, to no avail. By now he was starting to panic. He phoned his cousin, Bill Muldock, who came with his tools. Harvey watched from the sidelines, pacing back and forth, while Bill poked and prodded the engine, eventually diagnosing a bad generator.

He phoned various auto parts suppliers, who were singularly unhelpful, pointing out that generators for a 1951 Plymouth Cranbrook convertible were not in abundant supply. He finally phoned a company in California that thought they had one, but weren't sure, so they'd have to get back to him. The next Sunday he was in church, on his knees, beseeching the Lord to intervene and heal his car.

His prayers were answered the week before the parade, when they called from California to tell him they'd found a generator in Montana and they'd be shipping it out just as soon as they received it. He mentioned this at the Monday night meeting of the Odd Fellows, when Clevis Nagle asked if the Cranbrook would be up and running in time for the parade. Harvey wasn't sure, but he didn't think so.

Well, Clevis said, they couldn't have the parade without the Cranbrook! Where would the Sausage Queen sit, after all? She couldn't very well walk the parade route now, could she? No, this wouldn't do. This wouldn't do at all.

They voted to postpone the parade until Harvey could assume his rightful place at the head of the line. This did not go over well with the masses, who wanted to know who had died and left the Odd Fellows in charge. So Kyle Weathers, this year's president of the lodge, held a press conference in which he reminded the citizenry that the Corn and Sausage Days festival was begun by the Odd Fellows in 1953 and that they would hold it whenever and wherever they wished, thank you.

But this year's real story was the selection of Clevis's granddaughter, Tiffany Nagle, as the Sausage Queen. It was a close contest. She was running neck and neck with Amanda Hodge, right up until the essay portion of the contest, when Amanda read her essay about the implications of Newtonian physics, while Tiffany speculated how wonderful it would be if everyone loved one another, then pledged that if chosen as the Sausage Queen, she would devote her reign to working for world peace. As soon as she said that, Amanda was toast.

There has never been great interest in our town in Newtonian physics, though to be honest people aren't much for world peace either. It is the general consensus that there won't be peace until Jesus returns on the clouds in glory to ransom his elect. Therefore, any efforts to achieve world peace are viewed with suspicion, as a plot by the United Nations to usurp the sovereignty of God.

But the men of the Odd Fellows Lodge, who judge the contest, were moved by Tiffany's selflessness, or so they said. It also helped that in Tiffany's eighteenth summer, God had seen fit to bless her with a stunning physique. Newtonian physics was good, as far as it went, but Tiffany Nagle in a clingy gown talking about loving one another was a tough act to follow.

She was the second Nagle to win the Sausage Queen contest. Her aunt Nora had won it in 1974, before going on to capture the state Sausage Queen title the next year, then moving to New York and starring in an underwear commercial as a dancing grape. It isn't easy growing up in a family of overachievers, and Nora's shadow has loomed over Tiffany since she was a child. An ordinary person might break under the strain, but it's only made Tiffany stronger and more determined than ever to continue the Nagle legacy.

The generator for Harvey's car arrived the Wednesday before the rescheduled parade. The transplant was planned for the next evening. His cousin Bill operated while Harvey passed him the tools and wiped the sweat from his brow. Meanwhile, the Odd Fellows were gathered for a prayer vigil at the lodge, exhorting the Lord to guide

Bill's hands. After two hours, the generator was successfully installed, Harvey turned the key, and the engine roared to life.

He began to weep, sitting in his car, thinking about how close he'd come to losing his beloved Cranbrook. He phoned the lodge to report the good news, then waxed the Cranbrook to ready it for the parade.

The next day he drove to Tiffany Nagle's house to prepare her for the festivities. He showed her where in the Cranbrook to sit (feet on the backseat, buttocks on the trunk), how to wave to the crowds (palm in, a slight rotation of the hand at the wrist), and when to place her hand over her heart (during the recitation of the town poem and while passing the home of the late Horace Huffman, founder of the Harmony chapter of the Odd Fellows in 1929).

With the delay of the Chicken Noodle Dinner, the Friendly Women's Circle used the two extra weeks to sand and paint the kitchen cabinets, since it appears they won't be buying new cabinets in the foreseeable future. After two years, their Cabinet Fund had reached $53.78, which put them on a pace to have new cabinets sometime around the year 2375. So they took the $53.78 and went to Grant's Hardware and bought paint instead.

Since Quakers don't vote, but rather prayerfully discern the will of God, it took them three meetings to determine the Lord preferred pale yellow cabinets. I helped them paint. They had been hinting I should be more supportive of the Circle and its ministry. Fern Hampton had lately been reminiscing about Pastor Taylor's devotion to their noble cause. "Every Tuesday morning, there he was at the noodle table, flour up to his elbows, rolling out noodles. What a godly example he was. There isn't a day that goes by that I don't mourn his passing. He's the finest man of God I ever knew." This comes as an utter shock to those who remember that, when Pastor Taylor was alive, Fern tried three times to have him fired.

By the day of the parade, the cabinets were painted and the ladies of the Circle were good to go. Concerned my initial blessing had worn off, they asked me to pray over the noodles again, which I did, albeit reluctantly. Public prayer has never been my strong suit, as I have grave doubts about its appropriateness, prayer being something Jesus advised us to do privately, in our closets. I borrow most of my prayers from books, but though I looked far and wide, I couldn't find a noodle prayer and had to make up my own.

"Uh, thank you, Lord, for these noodles, and for the wheat of the field which gives us flour. Thank you for your creation, especially the chickens who laid the eggs so we can make our noodles, and for the, uh," I paused, trying to recall the other ingredients of noodles.

"Salt and water," Fern interrupted. "Flour, eggs, salt, and water."

"And thank you for salt and water, and for the hands which prepared these noodles. Amen."

"Amen," the Friendly Women echoed.

"Now, Pastor Taylor, that man knew how to pray," Fern said. "When he got done praying, those noodles knew they'd been prayed over. You might want to work on that, Sam."

I assured her I would.

I left the noodle blessing and walked down Washington Street to the elementary school to watch people line up for the parade. My father was sitting astride our 1939 Farmall Model M tractor, just behind Harvey Muldock and Tiffany Nagle, resplendent in her Sausage Queen gown and tiara.

At the stroke of eleven, Darrell Furbay blasted the fire siren, the signal for everyone to fall in line and pipe down. Tiffany rose from her Cranbrook throne and was escorted to the podium, next to the victory bell in front of the school, where she thanked her parents for their support, pledged her commitment to world peace, then recited the town poem written in 1898 by Harmony's poet laureate, Ora Crandell. She paused after that to dab her eyes, blow her nose, and regain her composure.

"I also want to thank the pork producers for my one-hundred-dollar scholarship, and even though I'm a vegetarian, I am honored to serve as your Sausage Queen and promise never to tarnish the reputation of your organization."

People turned and stared at one another, aghast.

"What'd she just say?" Kyle Weathers asked me.

"That she's a vegetarian, but that she'll never tarnish the reputation of the pork producers."

"A vegetarian!" he shrieked. "She's the Sausage Queen, for cryin' out loud. She can't be a vegetarian. It's against the rules."

There were scattered boos throughout the audience. A sausage patty was lobbed through the air, just missing Tiffany but striking Harvey Muldock square on the chest. Clevis Nagle threw his coat over Tiffany to protect her and hustled her off the stage and into Harvey's car, which sped away, the Sausage Queen banner flapping in the wind.

My father, in a valiant effort to salvage the parade, crank-started the Farmall and headed north on Washington Street with Bernie the policeman and the high-school band following in his wake. Unfortunately, Tiffany's shocking revelation had dulled the crowd's enthusiasm and most of them left for home, not even bothering to stop past the meetinghouse for the Chicken Noodle Dinner. Who could eat at a time like this?

Not being an Odd Fellow, I wasn't present at the emergency meeting they held to discuss Tiffany's scandalous disclosure, though the next day at church Harvey Muldock told me what happened.

"The pork producers are threatening to pull their scholarship unless Tiffany renounces vegetarianism and eats a sausage link in public."

"That's ridiculous. They can't take back her scholarship."

"They sure can," Harvey said. "Tiffany signed a paper that she'd promote pork products and how can she do that if she's a vegetarian? They want her to resign and Amanda Hodge to take her place."

But that wasn't the worst of it. The Chicken Noodle Dinner had been a bust, with fifty-three quarts of chicken and noodles left unsold. Fern Hampton was fit to be tied. "Why'd she have to go and say she was a vegetarian. She ruined it for everybody. I tell you, the kids these days think only of themselves. Selfishness, pure selfishness. She oughta be ashamed."

I made the observation that vegetarianism was a dietary choice, not a mortal sin.

"And I lay this directly at your feet, Sam Gardner. You've been winking at sin ever since you got here and now look what's happened. The Chicken Noodle Dinner is in ruins and our church is near collapse. If this isn't the judgment of the Lord against you, I don't know what is."

I apologized to Fern for not preaching more against vegetarianism, then excused myself to go home.

A night's rest did not improve her disposition. She was still cranky at the Monday night meeting of the Christian Education Committee. On Tuesday, I learned Tiffany had been dethroned, and the Sausage Queen crown offered to Amanda Hodge, who kindly refused it, electing to side with the despised and oppressed.

I mentioned it to my wife at the supper table.

"That's pretty sad," she said.

"How so?" I asked.

"Amanda Hodge is sixteen and gets the point. Fern is seventy-five, has been attending church all her life, and is dense as a brick."

I thought about that for a moment. "It's probably not that simple. Fern cares about the church. She's just forgotten its purpose."

"I wish she'd remember it," Barbara said. "It'd make life a whole nicer."

"But not nearly as interesting."

I went for a walk that evening. We were on autumn's doorstep. It was getting darker earlier. A dead leaf skittered across the sidewalk in front of me, rattling like bones, pushed by a northern wind. As I walked, I reflected on parades, churches, Odd Fellows, and organizations in general, how we start with such noble purposes, but come to care more about our perpetuation than we do the noble passions that first united us. Thus, free-thinkers and vegetarians are always a threat and can be cast aside in our misguided quest for purity.

I'm not usually given to such contemplation. It made me tired and a little depressed, so I turned toward home and returned to my sons, who will one day have their own quests, but for now seem thankfully immune to the lure of self-preservation.

Thirteen

Hope Blossoms

With the impeachment of Tiffany Nagle, life in Harmony has gone to Hades in a handbasket, to quote my wife. There was no one to sing the national anthem at the first football game, so Bea Majors sang, which is an appalling way to begin any endeavor. It not only turned the town against music; our football team lost by forty-three points.

When Kivett's Five and Dime held their fall sale, there was no Sausage Queen to model the latest fashions. Consequently, sales were off 15 percent and Ned Kivett was in a tizzy.

Then the nursing home added a new wing and without the Sausage Queen to cut the ribbon, they invited Pastor Jimmy at the Harmony Worship Center to say a few words. He ended up preaching for half an hour, wrapping up the proceedings with an altar call and reminding the audience they could end up in that very nursing home the next day, off their rocker, unable to accept God's gift of salvation.

"You think these nursing homes stink? They smell like roses compared to hell," he said. "You might want to give that some thought."

You can't hand the microphone to someone like Pastor Jimmy if you haven't built it into the schedule and aren't prepared to carry the additional baggage. A Sausage Queen smiles, says a few words about world peace, cuts the ribbon, then hands the ceremonial scissors back to the emcee, who gets the show on the road. They know when to speak and when to be quiet, a talent that eludes certain ministers, Pastor Jimmy being one of them.

A petition began circulating, demanding the Odd Fellows reinstate Tiffany as the Sausage Queen before people revolted, the town descended into anarchy, and Western civilization was irreparably damaged. But the Odd Fellows held their ground, being the principled men they are, and demanded that Tiffany first disavow vegetarianism, which she refused to do. They were locked in a stalemate, with no end in sight.

Harvey Muldock asked me to intervene and mediate the dispute, over Kyle Weathers's objections, who said I was a known Democrat and a closet vegetarian. He'd worked the polls last May, and when I'd declared my political affiliation, he'd tried for half an hour to sway me toward the Republicans, citing a long list of Democratic misdeeds dating back to Thomas Jefferson and his mistress.

I vote Democrat for religious reasons, as a form of self-flagellation. Some Christians beat themselves with whips during Lent to demonstrate their penance. I vote Democrat in a town of Republicans, enduring the contempt of my peers for the sake of our Lord, who, like most people of Jewish persuasion, was also a Democrat.

Besides Jesus and me, there are two other Democrats in our town—Mabel and Deena Morrison. It has been rumored for several years that Miriam Hodge leans toward liberalism after she'd donated a book about Jimmy Carter to the public library, but her political affiliation has yet to be verified, though not for lack of trying. Dale Hinshaw routinely insists that Miriam, as a church elder, disclose her political leanings, lest she have nefarious intentions of infiltrating the congregation with fellow travelers.

With the fall elections a scant month away, the ouster of Tiffany Nagle has become the eye of the storm. Mabel Morrison is running for town council on the Democratic ticket and has rallied to Tiffany's side. She is running against Harvey Muldock, who would be more than happy to leave the council, but hates the thought of going down in history as the first man in town to lose his seat to a liberal, and a woman at that.

Mabel is garnering a fair share of support from the other women in town, who are tired of the men bungling things. The men, being men, have been spending money on a new town garage, even though the old garage was perfectly fine. It's the school that needs repairing, but try telling that to the men on the council, who are of the opinion that if Abraham Lincoln learned to write in a log cabin using a slate slab and a hunk of charcoal, it's good enough for our children.

The Tiffany Nagle scandal might be costing Clevis Nagle his marriage, which wasn't a good marriage to start with, but now is worse. He and his wife, Viola, come to my office at least once a month, their union on the verge of fracture. It used to worry me, until Miriam Hodge pointed out they'd been bickering the entire forty-two years of their marriage.

"It's Viola," Miriam explained. "She's one of these people who always need a crisis. If it isn't her marriage, it's something else. Don't let her draw you in. Just smile and tell her you're praying for her."

Clevis is a member of the town council, and a rather timid one at that. His wife kept waiting for him to step in and defend their granddaughter, but he's kept his finger in the air gauging the political wind. So Viola began campaigning for Mabel Morrison, going door to door and passing out brochures, which has incensed the Republicans. No one opens their door for Mabel, she being a Democrat and it being election time. When they see her on their doorstep, they pretend no one's home. But when Viola knocks, they assume she's campaigning for the Republicans and open the door. It is a variation on the Trojan horse strategy. Once the door is open, they're busted. Viola doesn't leave until they've promised to vote for Mabel.

As far back as I can remember, controversy has swirled around this town. I think it has to do with our size and isolation. Disagreement and bickering are the only entertainment options available to us. It would help if we had cable television, which will never happen because Uly Grant donates a hundred dollars to each town council member's campaign with the understanding they won't allow cable, which would cut into his antenna sales.

Grant's Hardware is the closet thing Harmony has to a political-action committee. The members of the town board—Clevis Nagle, Harvey Muldock, and Owen Stout—gather there and eat donuts in Uly's office.

I happened to be there buying a new showerhead for my basement shower and saw them troop past the nail bin toward Uly's office to discuss the Mabel Morrison threat. I edged closer, pretending to be interested in the canning jars stacked next to the door.

"Why don't you get your brother-in-law to arrest her?" I heard Clevis suggest to Harvey. "She rolls right through the stop sign in front of our house. Maybe a month in the pokey will take the wind out of her sails."

"You can't arrest someone for rolling through a stop sign," Owen pointed out. "Now if she ran over somebody, that would be a different matter entirely."

None of them being willing to get run over, they batted other ideas back and forth aimed at discrediting Mabel—putting empty whiskey bottles on the curb outside her home on trash-pickup day, writing a letter to the editor in support of same-gender marriage and signing her name to it, anonymously donating a sex manual to the public library in her honor.

I crept past the plumbing fixtures to the checkout and asked Uly if I could borrow his phone. It took three phone calls to track down Mabel at the Legal Grounds to tell her that canning supplies were on sale at Grant's Hardware and she'd better hurry before everything was sold.

I was lurking behind the bolt bin when Mabel walked in five minutes later. She made her way to the canning supplies, but stopped short when she overheard her name.

"We could run a personals ad in the *Herald*," Clevis Nagle was saying. "*Widowed woman looking for a good time with no strings attached.* Then we could put Mabel's phone number in there. That'd sink her boat."

Mabel frowned.

The men discussed other ideas to tarnish Mabel's reputation, before moving on to discuss various matters of town business. I watched as Mabel reached into her purse and pulled out a disposable camera. She stepped into the office doorway and snapped a picture just as they were raising their hands to vote.

"My, isn't this interesting," Mabel said. "The town council appears to be having a meeting without first posting a notice in the newspaper, a direct violation of the state's open-door law. Wait till people hear about this."

And with that, she turned and walked out.

Clevis Nagle leaped to his feet. "Eavesdropper!" he cried out after her. "Snake in the grass!"

To the outsider, this behavior might seem extreme, though it is par for the course for our town at election time. Accusations and scandals swirl about like starlings in fall, agitating the populace. After the election, the dust settles, the issues are stored away until the next election, and a certain complacency falls upon the town like soft snow. But October is a bitter month, and this one was no different.

The next day, Mabel made copies of the picture and posted them all over town, demanding the town council be imprisoned. The battle spilled over into my Sunday school class. When I pulled that week's question from the hat, it read, "Can Democrats be true Christians or must they repent first?"

It was Dale Hinshaw's handwriting.

A pitched battle ensued, with Mabel and Deena Morrison surrounded on all sides. I didn't take an official position. These people have long memories, and my annual review was a scant six months away. But I wasn't the only one holding back. Dr. Pierce was unusually quiet and clearly uncomfortable.

"We could use a little help, honey," Deena said, smiling at Dr. Pierce, who smiled back, though rather weakly.

"Oh, Lord," Mabel Morrison groaned. "He's a Republican."

"I knew there was something about him I liked," Dale Hinshaw said. "I shoulda figured it out. He's a doctor and all your doctors are Republicans." He leaned back in his chair, folded his arms across his chest, and smiled triumphantly.

"You never told me a you were a Republican," Deena said.

"You never asked."

"Oh, Lord, my granddaughter's going to have a mixed marriage," Mabel wailed.

"Isn't that just like a Democrat?" Stanley Farlow said. "They're all for diversity until it comes to Republicans marrying into the family."

"Who said anything about getting married?" Deena asked. "I'm not getting married."

Dr. Pierce turned toward Deena. "You don't want to marry me?"

"You haven't asked."

"What would you say if I did?"

"I'm not sure," Deena said. "Why don't you ask me? Then we'll both know."

"I thought we were talkin' about whether or not Democrats had to repent," Dale said. "How come we never discuss my questions?"

"Pipe down," Mabel snapped. "My granddaughter's about to snag herself a husband."

The room quieted and everyone turned to look at Dr. Pierce, who, to his credit, blushed. "It isn't that I don't want to ask you. I simply envisioned a different scenario, perhaps something a bit more private."

"We don't mind," Mabel said.

"We can leave the room if you'd like," Uly Grant offered.

"Yes, why don't we," I said, standing and herding everyone to the door, then closing it behind me.

We gathered outside, around the door. Asa Peacock bent and peered through the keyhole.

"What's he doin'?" Dale asked.

"He's down on one knee, and he's saying something."

Mabel pushed him aside and put her mouth to the keyhole. "Deena, honey, now's your chance. Don't blow it." She pulled a handkerchief from her purse and dabbed her eyes. "I wish her grandfather had lived to see this."

I suggested we give them a bit more privacy.

"Shhh," Mabel hissed. "I can't hear what he's saying."

The door swung open, and Mabel toppled to the floor.

"Does anyone here have a ring I could borrow?" Dr. Pierce asked.

We all had wedding rings, but finger fat had grown around them over the years, preventing their removal.

Mabel spied a large ring on Dale's finger. "What's that ring, Dale?"

"That's my Mighty Men of God ring. I can't give that away. It's genuine gold-plated."

"Oh, stop your whining and give it to him," Mabel snapped. "You'll get it back just as soon as he gets to the store to get her a real one." She turned to Dr. Pierce. "You are going to buy her a real one, aren't you?"

"Most assuredly," he promised.

Dale eased the ring off his finger and looked at it longingly, then handed it to Dr. Pierce.

"I certainly appreciate this, Mr. Hinshaw," he said. "I'll be sure to return it. Sam, may I please borrow your pen?"

"Certainly," I said, reaching into my shirt pocket to retrieve it.

Then he stepped back into the room, closing the door behind him.

Mabel crouched down and squinted through the keyhole, using first one eye and then the other. "Daggone him, anyway," she said.

"What's wrong?" Dale asked.

"He put Sam's pen in the keyhole. I can't see a thing."

She folded the weekly church bulletin into a tube and placed the broad end against the door, fitting the other end into her ear. "He's asking her. Oh, sweet Jesus, I'm going to have great-grandchildren after all."

She listened for a moment, then rapped the door sharply with her knuckles. "Speak up, Deena honey. I can't hear you. What'd you say?"

She was greeted with silence. One minute passed, then two.

"Maybe he killed her," Asa Peacock said. "I seen something like this in a movie once. This man asked a lady to marry him in a grocery store and she said no and he told her if he couldn't have her, then no one would, and he choked her to death right then and there in the frozen foods."

Mabel panicked. She seized the doorknob and gave it a violent twist. The door flew open with a bang. Dr. Pierce and Deena were standing in the middle of the room, locked in an embrace and joined at the lips.

"Don't surprise me a bit," Dale observed. "The Democrats show up and before you know it, there's sex all over the place."

This is life in our town. The Sausage Queen is caught in a scandal, chaos ensues, and when the dust settles, a marriage is born. From the seeds of tragedy, hope blossoms.

A June wedding, I thought to myself. Outside. Maybe next to the Hodge's farm pond. Somewhere far away from electricity so Bea Majors couldn't play the organ. Dancing late into the evening to a chorus of crickets. The Sausage Queen, her dalliance with vegetarianism forgiven and forgotten, wearing her sash, twirling in the twilight.

fourteen

Desecration

We woke up the third Monday in October to a sunny, fall morning. It was my day off, a blank spot on the calendar with not one obligation.

"Do you want to do something today," my wife asked at the breakfast table.

I have been married long enough to know that when my wife asks if I want to do something, she isn't asking if I want to do something. She is letting me know she wants to do something.

But I was feeling feisty that morning and wanted to pester her a bit. "No, not really, but thanks for asking."

She picked up her dishes, walked over to the sink, and set them down harder than necessary.

"You know," she said after a while, "we don't have to stay home all the time. There's a great big world out there to see."

I decided to push her a little further. "I thought maybe we'd stay home so you could get caught up on the housework."

By now, the vein on her neck was standing out the way it does when she's mad, but doesn't speak for fear she'll lose control and choke the life out of me.

"Or," I said, "maybe we could see if my folks would watch the boys after school and you and I could drive over to McCormick's Creek, eat lunch at the inn, and go for a hike."

The vein in her neck began to throb less violently.

"Really?"

"Sure, why not. The laundry can wait until tonight."

"You're all heart, Sam."

The boys were less pleased. When I'd phoned my parents, I'd volunteered them to help my father rake leaves after school.

My parents have twenty-six large trees on their property. If you don't move quickly, it is entirely possible to be suffocated by falling leaves. My father has bought every leaf removal gadget known to humankind, without success. His life from mid-September to early November is one pitched battle after another. His yard resembles a battlefield, with the smoldering ruins of leaf piles and my father lying slumped against a tree, weary from combat. When not raking, he is peering frightfully out their parlor window, as a beaten general watches an approaching army, knowing his cause is lost but unwilling to surrender.

In contrast, I depend on the Lord for victory, letting my fallen leaves remain on the ground, trusting that God in his grace will send a wind that will blow them into my neighbor's yard.

It took an hour to reach McCormick's Creek. We went the back roads, striking out through the country in a northerly direction, through Greene County and up into Owen County, crossing the river at Freedom on the last ferry in Indiana, which runs in the spring and fall, saving the farmers from having to drive their equipment twenty miles around to the bridge in Spencer.

My wife has never been fond of water and, while on the ferry, sat in the car with the seat belt cinched tightly across her lap, gripping the dashboard with whitened knuckles. The ferryman stood outside her window, pointing out half-submerged logs, undertows, and other natural dangers that could at any moment plunge us to a watery grave.

Despite the ferryman's dire predictions, the crossing was uneventful. Twenty minutes later, we arrived at the state park, paid our entrance fee, and drove to the inn for a fried-chicken dinner. We spent the rest of the day hiking, then at dusk made our way back to the car for the trip home.

We hadn't gone five miles when an animal darted in front of us and was punished for its poor timing with a solid whack from my bumper.

"What was that?" my wife asked, startled from her slumber.

I eased over to the side of the road. "I'm not sure. I think it was a dog. I wonder if I killed it."

Whatever it was was lying by the side of the road, motionless. I could barely make it out in the dark, but it appeared to be a dog. Barbara came up beside me with a blanket.

"What is it?"

"I think it's a dog, but whatever it is, it has spots."

"I hope it isn't a Dalmatian." My wife is inordinately fond of Dalmatians, having sat through several dozen showings of *101 Dalmatians* with our sons.

"I'm not sure what it is. Let's get it into the lights." I wrapped the blanket around it and carried it to the front of the car so I could see it with the headlights. Barbara pulled back the blanket, gasped, and jumped back. "It's a bobcat," she said, thoroughly amazed. "I didn't even know they were around here."

"It was probably someone's pet. It's wearing a collar."

She asked if it was dead.

I placed my hand on its rib cage. "No, it's still breathing, but just barely."

"What do you suppose we should do?"

"Take it to a vet, I guess."

At the next town, we pulled over at a gas station and asked directions to the veterinarian's office, which was closed. By then, the bobcat had expired.

"You killed it," my wife said.

"Not on purpose."

"If you hadn't been driving so fast, it might have lived."

"I was only going forty."

"What should we do with it?" she asked.

"Have Ernie Matthews stuff it, so we can put it in the living room?" I suggested.

"Fat chance."

"Then I think we should take it home and bury it."

We transferred it to the trunk of the car, then drove home in a quiet mood, mulling over the brevity of life.

"Why don't you let me off at your folks and the boys and I can walk home while you bury it," my wife suggested as we approached town. "That way they won't have to know their father is a killer."

I dropped her off at my parents, then went home, and began rooting through the garage looking for a shovel. The phone rang before I found it. It was Bea Majors, telling me her sister Opal was in the hospital in Cartersburg and had requested my presence.

Opal Majors is a notorious hypochondriac and routinely imagines she has all types of exotic illnesses. In the four years I've been her pastor, she claims to have been afflicted with the bubonic plague, scarlet fever, jungle rot, and the Ebola virus. The drawback to being a hypochondriac is that when you really are ill, no one believes you. Opal had been sick for a month, but whenever she told anyone, they changed the subject.

Now she was awaiting emergency heart surgery. I left a note for my wife and hurried to the hospital. I found Opal propped up in bed, positively elated. "I've been telling everyone I was sick. Now maybe people will believe me. Three clogged arteries, one of them 100 percent. If Bea hadn't come along when she did, I'd be dead right now. No telling what all they'll find when they open me up. I'm probably full of cancer too."

I prayed my standard prayer for someone about to be operated on, then sat with Bea while they wheeled Opal away to surgery. I was there most of the night before the doctor came out to tell us she'd come through the operation in good shape. I went home to get a few hours sleep, then left for the meetinghouse.

It had turned cold overnight, a harbinger of winter. The weatherman on the car radio was predicting lows in the upper teens, unusually cold for October, but not unheard of.

The day was a busy one, with three meetings, a handful of house visits, and another trip to Cartersburg to visit Opal, who was sitting up in bed, ordering the nurse to check her blood for lyme disease, which she'd just read about in a magazine.

She brightened when she saw me. "Oh, Sam, I'm so glad you're here. Can you say a word of prayer for me? I have a feeling I'm not long for this world."

"But Opal, your doctor said the operation went well, and that you'll be going home tomorrow."

"Of course he's gonna say that. You think he's gonna admit he botched the operation? I tell you, Sam, something is terribly wrong with me. I can feel it." She clutched my hand. "Promise me you'll have Miriam Hodge sing 'Abide with Me' at my funeral."

I assured her I would.

"And make sure Johnny Mackey gets me in the right plot."

"I'll make sure of it."

"Thank you, Sam, you've been a good pastor to me."

"I'm glad you think so."

"Will you make sure Sniffles gets a good home?" Sniffles was her cat.

"She can come live with us," I promised.

She went over her funeral in great detail before I could make my escape. I got home just in time for supper, then played a board game with the boys, read them a story, and put them to bed. Barbara and I stayed up to watch the news from the city.

The newscaster led with the weather, advising people to have their furnaces checked, then related that day's mayhem, and closed by interviewing a man from the Department of Natural Resources.

It had been a long day, and I was half asleep. I only heard half the words. ". . . released near McCormick's Creek State Park wearing a radio transmitter collar . . . we've tracked it to Harmony . . . Cartersburg . . . the bobcat . . . and then back to Cartersburg . . . now somewhere near the town of Harmony. Persons killing an endangered species can receive up to a year in prison and a ten-thousand-dollar fine. If viewers see the bobcat, please phone the sheriff's department. Meanwhile, it is recommended that pets be kept inside."

I was considerably revived by now and listening closely to the television.

"What did you do with that bobcat?" Barbara asked.

I tried to think how best to answer.

"Were you in Cartersburg today?"

I nodded meekly.

"Did you bury it?"

I shook my head no.

Thankfully, the phone rang, saving me from my wife's inquisition. It was Opal, calling from the hospital. "There's a bobcat on the loose. Go get Sniffles."

I promised Opal I'd guard Sniffles with my life.

"Call the sheriff," Barbara demanded, after I'd hung up the phone.

"Are you crazy? Did you hear what they said? A year in prison and a ten-thousand-dollar fine for killing an endangered species."

"It was an accident. They won't do anything to you."

"I'd rather not take my chances."

"We have to do something. You can't carry it around in the trunk of our car."

"I'll just have to bury it, I suppose."

"And just where will you bury it that won't get someone else in trouble?"

I thought for a moment, then was struck with a brilliant idea. "In Opal Major's plot at the graveyard. She won't be needing it anytime soon. Besides, she loves cats."

Fortunately, it was cold and the bobcat hadn't begun to stink. I found the shovel outside, leaning against a tree near where the boys had dug for treasure. I drove the back streets to the cemetery, keeping an eye peeled for any cars that might be following. I parked my car at the Co-op across the street from the cemetery and climbed the fence, the bobcat draped across my shoulders like a mink stole.

I removed the sod carefully, setting it aside for later use. I dug down three feet, then laid the bobcat to rest, the blanket protecting its body from the dirt. I filled the hole, replaced the sod, then dumped the extra soil on Albert Finchum's grave, who'd died the week before.

It never occurred to me to remove the radio collar, which is how the Department of Natural Resources found the bobcat two days later, after Opal gave permission for them to exhume her grave. She wasn't the least bit surprised. "That's what comes from having a funeral director who's blind as a bat. He's been burying people in the wrong graves for years," she told anyone who'd listen. "There's no telling who they'll find in there."

Dead Bobcat Found in Opal Majors's Grave read the headline of that week's edition of the *Harmony Herald*. Bob Miles speculated it was the work of a deranged teenager who'd gotten caught up in a cult involving Satanic worship and animal sacrifice.

Letters to the editor flooded into the paper decrying today's youth and demanding jail time for anyone caught desecrating a grave. The fact that Opal wasn't in it at the time seemed to escape them. Pastor Jimmy at the Harmony Worship Center held a youth rally and brought in a Christian weightlifting team who spoke about the heavy burden of sin, then encouraged the youth to build up their spiritual muscles and bench-press for the Lord.

The last week of October, the sheriff went on television and offered amnesty to any teenager who confessed. "Basically, we're just concerned that this person, whoever he or she may be, get help." He looked directly into the camera and made a personal appeal to the bobcat killer. "Right now you're probably scared and confused, but it's not too late. We can help you. Just turn yourself in before the urge to kill again gets stronger. Today, it's a bobcat. But tomorrow, it could be your own mother. Call us now, before it's too late."

Having no intention of running over my mother, I ignored his plea. Ignoring my wife wasn't quite as simple. She reminded me confession was good for the soul. Although it might be good for the soul, it can be disastrous for the reputation. Instead, I took my counsel from the Bible: *There is a time to keep silent and a time to speak* (Ecclesiastes 3:7). And if this wasn't a time to keep silent, I didn't know what was.

Fifteen

Autumn Leaves

*H*arvey Muldock lost the town council election by one vote to Mabel Morrison and, from all outward appearances, was ecstatic. He sauntered into the Coffee Cup the morning after the election and instructed Vinny to pour everyone a cup of coffee, that the drinks were on him. Unfortunately, this did little to improve the mood of the patrons, who'd interpreted Harvey's loss as an affront to their God-given right to rule the town. As nearly as they could figure, there weren't enough women in town to ensure Mabel's victory, which meant several men had forsaken their commitment to the male gender. They'd spent the morning speculating who the traitors might be.

I hope they don't find me out. I hadn't gone to the polls intending to vote for Mabel, but the prospect of new blood on the town council intrigued me and at the last moment I found my finger flicking the lever over her name.

I've always had a fondness for Mabel Morrison, ever since I was a child and would walk with my mother four blocks to Morrison's

Menswear the last week of August to buy back-to-school shoes. Her husband, Harold, would measure my foot, then wrestle it into a Red Goose shoe, while Mabel looked on from behind the cash register next to the red goose on the checkout counter, which dispensed a golden egg with every shoe purchase.

I associate Mabel with that pleasant enterprise—reaching up and pulling down the goose neck, listening to the rumble of a goose egg as it made its way through the goose entrails and into my cupped hands: a large golden egg filled with toys, candy, and other secret treasures, all of them mine. I suppose voting for Mabel was my way of hoping she might offer our town one more marvelous surprise.

Well, it was a surprise, though whether it was marvelous depended on one's gender. The women in town seemed exceedingly pleased, while the men appeared despondent, except for Harvey Muldock, who was looking forward to having his life back.

After visiting the Coffee Cup, he stopped by Mabel's house to pass on the baton. They exchanged pleasantries, and then Harvey informed her she'd be taking over his duties—oversight of the water and sewer departments.

"Shirley Finchum called this morning," he said, as he handed over the key to the wastewater treatment plant. "The pump went out at the lift station last night and sewage backed up in her basement. I told her you'd be over today to give her a hand cleaning up." He presented her with a thick stack of papers. "This came in Monday's mail. They're the new government regulations on water standards. You'll need to read 'em before the next meeting. Anyway, congratulations on your victory. I hope you find public service a rewarding experience."

"Why do I have to clean Shirley's house?" Mabel asked. "Don't we have insurance for that kind of thing?"

"We sure do, but there's a two-thousand-dollar deductible. Which, if we take that out of the water and sewer budget, won't leave us enough money to open the swimming pool next summer. Trust me when I tell you never to close the pool. That upsets the mothers something terrible."

"I didn't run for office to clean up sewage," Mabel said.

"None of us did. It just kinda worked out that way. Anyway, best of luck to you, Mabel. If you have any questions, feel free to ask Clevis."

"The same Clevis who just last month was at Grant's Hardware plotting to have me arrested?"

"Yeah, well, sometimes he gets a little carried away during elections. But he's 100 percent behind you now."

"I don't want him behind me," Mabel said. "I want him in front of me, where I can keep an eye on him."

Harvey smiled, shook Mabel's hand good-bye, then walked down the street toward the meetinghouse, where he stopped to visit.

I was on the phone, so he settled himself into a chair opposite my desk to wait. He spied a paper clip on my desk, picked it up, and began straightening it out. I cut the phone call short and greeted him.

He said hello, then asked if I'd voted for him.

"I thought voting was supposed to be secret."

"That's what people always say whenever they didn't vote for you."

"Sorry about that, Harvey. I just thought a change would be good for the town."

"Don't feel bad, Sam. I voted for her too." He leaned back in the chair and sighed. "Boy, am I glad to be done with that. Don't ever run for public office, Sam. It's a thankless task. People expect you to be at their beck and call. The least little thing goes wrong and they call you to complain. And the meetings. If I never go to another meeting, it'll be too soon."

"I can't imagine having a job like that," I said.

Harvey has never appreciated irony, and my comment sailed directly over his head.

"How's the missus taking it?" I asked.

"Oh, she's upset. She told me I had to find something else to do on Monday nights, that she doesn't want me hanging around during her euchre club."

"Funny you should mention that. Dale's been thinking of starting a Monday evening Bible study. Think you'd be interested?"

Harvey glanced at his watch, "Oh my, look at the time. Eunice wanted me home fifteen minutes ago. Sam, it's been good seeing you. You take care now."

And with that, he was out the door.

This has been the usual response since Dale had announced the Sunday before that he'd be starting a Bible study. Like most people of his theological persuasion, he is convinced we are living in the final days, that Jesus will soon return to ransom the elect, which always, conveniently, includes him. He has been citing various events to bolster his argument that the end is near—an increase in earthquakes, wars in the Middle East, global epidemics, and Mabel Morrison running for town council.

I've been encouraging people to volunteer for the class, just to keep Dale off our backs. So far, no one has signed up, which fills me with dread. After four years of pastoring Harmony Friends, I've discovered life is easier when Dale is occupied with some noble venture that occupies his time.

It would only take two or three disciples to make him feel important. Two or three folks willing to absorb his lunacy without taking it too seriously. People who aren't susceptible to agitation or causes, who will nod their heads in agreement, then go home and forget everything he said. Maybe some kindly soul who is hearing-impaired.

My wife had driven to Cartersburg that day to buy winter coats for the boys. The prospect of eating lunch by myself held little appeal, so Frank and I knocked off work at noon and walked over to the Coffee Cup for a bite to eat. On the way over, we discussed the election. I could tell he felt uneasy.

Halfway there, he blurted out that he'd voted for Mabel. "I had no idea she'd win. I just didn't want her to not have any votes. Then she had to go and win by one vote. One measly vote, and it's all my fault."

I looked at him and shook my head. "I hope you've learned from this."

"I don't know what I was thinking," he said. "I never thought she'd win."

I put my arm around him. "Let's look on the bright side."

"What bright side?"

"At least we know who to blame when the town falls apart."

He frowned. "So who'd you vote for?" he asked.

"I thought voting was supposed to be secret."

"You rat! You voted for her too, didn't you?"

"No comment."

"I won't tell on you, if you don't tell on me."

"Deal," I said, reaching over to shake his hand.

The election was the talk of the Coffee Cup. Kyle Weathers was holding forth at the liars' table, underneath the swordfish, offering various conspiracy theories. "You take a look at the voter registration. I bet they got half those names from the cemetery, like they did up in Chicago and got JFK in the White House. That's how those Democrats work. I wouldn't give you fifty cents for the whole lot of 'em."

"Don't they have to do a recount when it's that close?" Vinny Toricelli asked.

"Don't have to," Owen Stout said. "Only if Harvey asks for it."

"I say we demand a recount," Kyle blustered.

"You can demand it all you want. But they only have to do it if Harvey requests it in writing."

"I don't think that's going to happen," I said. "Harvey stopped by my office this morning and he seemed pretty happy. He's already given Mabel the keys to the sewer treatment plant. He told me so himself."

"So who'd you vote for, Sam?" Kyle asked, eyeing me suspiciously.

"Who I voted for is a private matter."

"Traitor," he hissed, with a withering glance.

It went downhill from there. Kyle wanted to phone the White

House and demand an investigation into voter fraud. Frank said that would be like asking the fox to guard the hen house, and the battle raged. I sat there listening, eating my hamburger as quickly as I could and wishing I had gone shopping with my wife. That's how bad it was.

After lunch, I drove out to visit the Hodges. Miriam had gone to visit her sister, who was sick, so I helped Ellis bring in the last of the corn. He ran the combine while I drove the truck to the elevator in Cartersburg. It was pleasant work, driving the back roads through the country on a bright autumn day, the trees hugging the creek banks off in the distance across the stubbled fields.

The leaves had succumbed to the autumn chill, except for those on the sycamores and oaks, which are always the last to surrender. Not unlike certain people in our town, who see change coming and tighten their grip, unwilling to let go. They fight a losing battle, a contest whose result has already been determined.

When I was in Miss Fishbeck's sixth-grade class, she told a story I've never forgotten, of Japanese soldiers on isolated Pacific islands who, never having learned of the combat's conclusion, continued waging a war whose end had been decided long before. Miss Fishbeck said that when some of the soldiers were told they'd lost, they didn't believe it and fought to their death.

At first, I thought she was making it up and I didn't believe her. Now that I'm older, I don't doubt it a bit. There are people in this town who want things to remain as they were in the 1950s, people still upset with Mabel Morrison for closing down the menswear store after Harold died, and don't vote for her for that reason. They want Ike to be president, and school to begin with prayer, which won't ever happen again, and they can't bear it. So they load their rhetorical guns to fight for a cause that is already lost.

Dale lives in a world that science disproved two centuries ago. He believes earthquakes are a sign of God's displeasure, not shifts in the earth's tectonic plates. Kyle thinks women are unsuited for leadership, which explains why no woman will marry him. They are oak leaves hanging on through spring, unwilling to make way for new life and fresh forms.

I thought about this on the way to the grain elevator, driving along in Ellis Hodge's grain truck, which doesn't have a radio and thus encourages reflection.

It took forty-five minutes to reach the elevator, and another half hour to unload and do the paperwork. I hadn't been there since I was a teenager and worked for Ellis on the weekends during the harvest. It hadn't changed much. A half dozen old men were clustered in the office, yellow flypaper speckled with last summer's kill hung from the ceiling, and a Sunny Morning heating stove occupied the center of the room. License plates dating back fifty years were nailed to the walls.

It is easy to understand the appeal of a place like this. These old men settle in their chairs at night, watching news of an alien world they no longer understand. The elevator is their last fraying link to a world they knew and understood and wished they could reclaim, but can't. They are old soldiers, making their last stand while the enemy circles outside.

Driving back to the Hodges' farm, I wonder if this might be

God's way of nudging me into the future. I picture myself old and embittered, at odds with the world, and the thought appalls me. If statisticians can be believed, my life is half lived. I don't want to spend this last half trying to recapture the first half. I want to stretch and grow and do bold things, like vote for Mabel Morrison and question what I've been taught and generally alarm people with my broad-mindedness.

By the time I made it back to the farm, Miriam was home. Ellis had finished the last field and was driving the combine into the equipment shed. They invited me to stay for supper, which I declined. I wanted to go home and see my sons and hear about their day.

The march toward winter has whittled down the daylight, and it was almost dark when I pulled into our driveway. My sons were watching for me from the kitchen window and came hurtling out the door, swarming around me like a great cloud of gnats.

It was a good way to end the day, surrounded by life and vigor. These spring-leaf sons of mine, bursting out and growing, reminding me that life isn't to be found in holding on and looking back, but in letting go and looking forward.

S i x t e e n

Heather

$\mathcal{T}$he rumor was first heard on a Monday morning in mid-November at the Coffee Cup Restaurant, where most of the town's rumors have their origins. Within an hour, it had made its way a block north to the *Harmony Herald* newspaper office, where Bob Miles sat, despondent over this bitter turn of events. He phoned Vinny at the Coffee Cup. "Is it true?"

"'Fraid so," Vinny said, his voice trembling with grief.

Bob hung up the phone and rested his head on the desk, wracked with sorrow.

Heather Darnell was leaving the Coffee Cup. His lovely, beautiful Heather. And not just his lovely, beautiful Heather. Everyone's lovely, beautiful Heather. Or at least all the old men at the Coffee Cup who planned their days around her work hours. Now they were beyond consolation. Heather was the wife they'd never had, but maybe could have had if they had paid as much attention to their wives as they had to Heather.

By lunchtime, the men of the Coffee Cup were in a dismal mood and, looking for someone to blame, had turned on Vinny. "She'd still be here if you weren't so cheap," Kyle Weathers said. "We kept tellin' you to give her a raise, but did you listen to us? No, you didn't. And now look where it's got us."

"Don't blame me. If you hadn't been such a lousy tipper, maybe she'd still be around."

I sat in the corner eating my lunch. I had been avoiding the place in order to preserve my arteries, but had lately been craving grease and had caved in. I was also there because my wife was mad at me and had suggested I fix my own meals for a while. That too had to do with Heather, who'd come to my office the week before seeking counsel. My wife had seen her enter the meetinghouse and later that day had inquired about her visit. I couldn't elaborate, of course, because it was confidential, which riled my wife even further.

My wife is not ordinarily the jealous type, but there is something about Heather Darnell that causes even the most self-assured woman to feel threatened.

She is twenty years old and her friends from high school are away at college. They come back for the summer, walk by the Coffee Cup, tap on the glass, and wave. But she no longer gets invited to all their parties, and when she does, they talk about their sororities and how they can't wait to finish college and move to the city, far away from this place.

They make fun of the town and the people in it and, she suspects, talk about her behind her back for still living here and working at the Coffee Cup. Or so she told me.

I'd asked her how she felt about working there. "It's okay, I guess. Everyone's nice to me and everything. I just don't want to spend my life there, that's all."

She had broken up with her boyfriend, who'd gone to Bloomington to college and used to drive home every weekend to see her, but lately had been avoiding the trip. She had been thinking of moving to the city, getting an apartment, and finding a job.

"Why not?" I'd said at the time, not believing she'd do it.

As I reflect back, I think my being a minister carried more weight with Heather than I'd considered. My approval of her plan was apparently just the nudge she needed. Within the week, she'd turned in her notice at the Coffee Cup and packed her bags.

The men at the Coffee Cup pleaded with her to stay, to no avail. Vinny offered to raise her pay twenty cents an hour and make her manager of the noon buffet, but to her credit she wouldn't be swayed by riches or titles. Several of the men offered to accompany her to the city and, though she seemed to appreciate their thoughtfulness, she declined their generous offers.

They held a going-away party for her on a Wednesday evening, Italian Night at the Coffee Cup. Bea Majors confused her nations and played *"Vaya Con Dios"* on the organ, poorly, missing most of the notes. Fortunately, Kyle Weathers was standing near the outlet and was able to nudge the organ's electrical cord loose with his foot.

Bob Miles had driven to the jeweler in Cartersburg to buy a brass plaque, which he hung over the buffet table, proclaiming it *The Heather Darnell Honorary Salad Bar and Buffet*. Five years before, it had been christened *The Doris Elmore Honorary Salad Bar and Buffet,* but that was a minor technicality and no one even pointed it out.

Heather gave a speech about how she would always remember the Coffee Cup for giving her a start in life. The old men began to weep, dabbing at their eyes with faded red bandanas they pulled from their back pockets. Vinny gave her a pen and pencil set from the Rexall drugstore, and the men presented her with a set of matching luggage they'd purchased at Kivett's Five and Dime.

Heather was outside the Rexall the next morning at ten-thirty, waiting for the bus to the city. Her parents were with her, along with a cluster of grief-stricken old men wearing their funeral suits, as if gathered for a wake. Bob Miles snapped a picture for the *Herald*.

They heard the bus before they saw it—a low, diesel rumble coming up the hill past the park. Then the bus heaved into sight near the Dairy Queen, its silver skin gleaming in the morning sun, a purveyor of suffering and woe.

Heather's father hugged her close, her mother kissed her good-bye, and the men lined up to shake her hand and pat her back. They gathered for one last group picture while the driver loaded Heather's new suitcases into the belly of the bus. Then Heather mounted the stairs and sat in the front seat, reaching her hand through the window to touch her parents one last time.

She came back that weekend for a visit, then Monday morning returned to the city to look for a job. She's staying with Shirley Finchum's niece and her husband, who have three small children and live in an old house on the north side, where all the rich people live. The agreement was for her to help with the kids four hours a day in exchange for a room in their basement.

She found a job at a restaurant where the waitresses wore skimpy

T-shirts that showed their belly buttons. She wore a sweater her first day, which the manager instructed her to remove so the customers could see her T-shirt. Heather doubted it was her T-shirt they wanted to see and said so. Then she asked why he didn't wear a T-shirt that showed his belly button, and that was when he let her go.

The next job, working as a cashier at a gas station, went a little better. She kept that job until noon, when the manager caught her talking people out of buying lottery tickets. She wanted to discuss whether it was right to encourage poor people to gamble. Unfortunately, her boss was not the philosophical type and promptly fired her.

Her third day in the city, she found a job at a McDonald's, working on the French fry line. By the next day, she had broken out in acne, wrenched her back after slipping on grease, and decided to take early retirement.

On the fifth day, she woke up early, packed her bags, and used the last of her money to buy a bus ticket back to Harmony. She worried the whole way home what her parents would think. The bus pulled up to the Rexall at four o'clock just as Kyle Weathers was closing his barbershop. He spied her out his front window and hurried outside to help with her luggage. He loaded it in the back of his truck and drove Heather home to her parents.

Mr. and Mrs. Darnell saw them turn off the highway and come down the driveway, Heather and Kyle in his Ford pickup. Her parents' worst nightmare—their beloved daughter throwing her life away on an old geezer like Kyle Weathers. She hadn't gone to the city to live. She'd run off to get married and now was coming home to tell them what she had done. She was pregnant and Kyle

Weathers was the father and they were going to get married and live in a trailer at the edge of town. And he would die when she was thirty-five, leaving her with nine children and a mortgage. She would have to go on food stamps and get a job tending bar at the Buckhorn. Their beautiful, precious daughter. All of those images flooded their minds as they watched Kyle climb from the truck, come around, open Heather's door, and carry in the luggage.

So when Heather told them the truth, that she'd gone through three jobs in four days and had come home and Kyle had been kind enough to give her a ride home from the bus stop, they were delirious with joy and not at all upset, as she had feared they would be. And though Heather was pleased with her reception, she couldn't understand it. But then who can figure parents?

She lay low the entire weekend, resting her back and scrubbing her face. Then on Monday morning she returned to the Coffee Cup to ask for her job back. Vinny was there by himself, frying bacon and making coffee. He didn't notice her come in. It was early; the morning crowd hadn't arrived yet. In fact, since Heather had left, there hadn't been a morning crowd. Or an afternoon or evening crowd for that matter.

Her apron was hanging on a hook next to the brass plaque. Bob Miles had framed a picture and placed it alongside the plague, over the phrase *Forever in Our Hearts*. It was the picture of her seated on the bus, looking through the window as it pulled away. She lifted down the apron and tied it around her waist.

"How about I start mixing the pancake batter?" she said.

Vinny spun around at the sound of her voice. He didn't speak at first. He tried, but words wouldn't come. "Is it really you?" he asked after a while.

"It's really me. And I might be available for employment again."

"Whatever it takes," Vinny said. "Name your price."

"A twenty-cent-an-hour raise and manager of the noon buffet."

"Done."

"Let's shake on it," Heather said, reaching out her hand.

So they shook on it.

"Maybe we oughta talk about you buying into the business," Vinny said. "A young person needs a stake in the future, and I'm not going to be around here forever."

"I don't have any money."

"Maybe you could ask your boss for loan. I think he'd be open to that suggestion."

"You'd do that for me?" Heather asked.

"For you," Vinny said, "I would do that."

It took thirty minutes for word to circulate among the elderly gentlemen in town that Heather was back to pouring coffee and consoling them in their old age. Within an hour, the Coffee Cup was full to overflowing. Men were peering through the window, praising God for this miraculous turn of events.

I stopped past around three, after the crowds had dwindled down. I ordered a Coke and made my way to a booth. Heather brought me my soda and sat down across from me.

"I see you're back," I said, stating the obvious.

"Yes, I'm back."

"So how do you feel? The last time we talked you didn't want to spend your life being a waitress."

Heather smiled. "I'm not a waitress. I'm an entrepreneur. Vinny is letting me buy into the business."

"That's wonderful, Heather. I'm happy for you. So how does it feel to be an entrepreneur?"

"Pretty good so far. Vinny's put me in the charge of the noon buffet and next week we're adding croutons and pineapple chunks."

I nodded my head solemnly. "Sounds like a fine place to start."

We sat quietly. I stirred my Coke, forming a tornado in the glass, while Heather surveyed the restaurant.

"Maybe now people won't think I'm a failure," she said after a while.

I continued stirring my Coke, then asked if she had ever seen the movie *It's a Wonderful Life*.

She thought for a moment. "Is that the one where the man jumps off a bridge and an angel takes him around town and shows him what it would have been like if he hadn't been born?"

"That's the one. Anyway, do you remember the end of the movie, when the angel says that no one is a failure who has friends?"

Heather nodded, then smiled. "You think that's true?"

"Yes, I do."

"What if she's only a waitress?" Heather asked.

"She's not. She's an entrepreneur."

We laughed. I rose to leave. "It's good having you back, Heather."

"It's nice to be back." She stood and I gave her a ministerial hug, not too tight and very brief, which made it all the more remarkable that my wife had chosen that very moment to walk past the Coffee Cup, glance through the window, and see us embracing.

"It was just a hug," I told her later that evening. "Nothing more. Purely innocent. I hug lots of women in the church." Which, in retrospect, was not the brightest thing to say.

I slept on the couch that night, thinking of the city, where morals are looser—women wear T-shirts that show their belly buttons and people gamble and ministers hug their parishioners and no one thinks a thing of it.

"I'm glad Heather's not there any longer. I'm glad she's back home, where people love her, some of them a little too much, to be sure, but in a harmless sort of way. And lying on the couch, listening to an occasional car driving past and Hester Gladden's dog barking in the distance, I thought of Heather and remembered what it was like to be young and full of dreams. I remember when I was her age, how my parents sent me off from home, hugging me close and telling me to shoot for the moon, that even if I missed, I'd end up among the stars.

Seventeen

Sam Finds His Backbone

Shirley Finchum had invited us to Thanksgiving at her house, with her two daughters and their families. This was their first Thanksgiving after Albert's passing. I knew it would be a glum day and was glad I already had plans.

I don't know Shirley well. She and her husband, Albert, began attending Harmony Friends back in August, when Albert caught a whiff of his mortality after being diagnosed with heart trouble. He was one of those people with impeccable timing who put God off all their lives, then at the very last moment sneak in the door—like the workers in the vineyard who arrived late but still received a full day's pay. I could tell it annoyed Dale Hinshaw, who griped that he had been laboring for the Lord sixty-three years and here came Albert Finchum, who got saved the week before he died and was even now lounging on a cloud while he, Dale, was left to inhabit this veil of tears.

I'd conducted Albert's funeral over the objections of his two daughters, who attended Harmony Worship Center and were concerned my presence at the funeral would undo their father's salvation after Pastor Jimmy had gone to all the trouble of getting him saved in the first place.

When Albert had begun attending Harmony Friends, he was hoping that washing dishes at the Chicken Noodle Dinner and mowing the churchyard a time or two would be enough to get him in God's good graces. It took Pastor Jimmy four home visits to set him straight, telling him if he weren't baptized in the name of Jesus he would roast in hell. And none of this sprinkling stuff like the Episcopalians and Catholics, Pastor Jimmy warned, but a good dunking in the stock tank behind the pulpit at the Harmony Worship Center. So Albert, anxious to cover all his bases, snuck off there one Sunday, got himself baptized in the name of Jesus, then returned to our meeting the next week, his sin purged.

A month later Albert Finchum shuffled off to glory. We held the funeral at the meetinghouse and buried him in the South Cemetery on Lincoln Street, across from the Co-op. The ladies of the Circle cooked the funeral dinner—ham, green beans, cheese potatoes, fruited Jell-O, lemonade or tea (mourner's choice), with pumpkin pie for dessert.

In lieu of flowers, donations were made to the meeting and we raised two hundred dollars, which the men of the church wanted to use to buy a memorial lawn mower, reflecting Albert's passion for lawn care. Albert's daughters wanted to use the money for a bookcase. The church quickly divided into lawn-mower and bookcase factions and likely would have split, until Miriam Hodge persuaded Uly Grant to knock twenty dollars off the price of a lawn mower and suggested to Albert's daughters that a bookcase made little sense in a church without books. So, instead, they purchased a book in their father's memory, which left enough money for the lawn mower, and a crisis was averted.

It took Albert's daughters several days to select a book befitting their father's stature in the community. They were torn between purchasing a Bible or a book about the Cincinnati Reds, Albert having been a big fan. After a round of arguing, they couldn't agree and compromised by buying a book they'd heard about on "Oprah"—a novel about women in the Bible.

Frank the secretary mentioned it in the church newsletter, along with a quote from me thanking the Finchum daughters for their generosity in donating this fine book, which I was confident would have a profound impact on anyone who read it. And though we were grieved by Albert's death, this book would remind us of his several weeks of selfless ministry to the church.

Fern Hampton signed it out the first Sunday it was available. No one heard or saw her for three days. She skipped the Christian Education meeting on Monday night and failed to show the next morning for the Friendly Women's Circle noodle making. When she did surface, in my office on Wednesday afternoon, she was livid.

"I'm just glad my mother isn't alive to see this," she said. "If she weren't dead, this would have killed her."

"What would have killed her?" I asked.

"The pastor encouraging us to read smut. Have you read that book the Finchum girls gave the church?"

"No."

"Well, maybe you should," she said. She shook her head in disgust. "Perversion. Nothin' but perversion. Full of filth. Sam Gardner, if the Lord doesn't strike you down, He ought to apologize to Sodom and Gomorrah, that's all I've got to say."

And with that she turned and stalked from my office.

I gave Fern several hours to calm down, then phoned her, asking if I could come by her house and get the book.

"Bea Majors has it. I told her all about it, and it upset her so much, she had to read it for herself."

Within a day, word of the book had spread through the Friendly Women's Circle, who, in the interests of maintaining community standards, vowed to read the book to judge whether the Finchum daughters should be drawn and quartered.

Later that week, Shirley Finchum was at the Kroger, where she ran into Miriam Hodge. Miriam hadn't read the book, but had been receiving a torrent of phone calls about it. And though she didn't want to add to a grieving widow's burden, she did think Shirley ought to know what had transpired, in the event her daughters were taken out by a Friendly Woman bent on purifying the world.

On Friday morning, Bea Majors passed the book on to her sister, Opal, who gave it to Hester Gladden, who read the first three chapters, was thoroughly scandalized, and in a fit of righteous indignation hauled it to the burn barrel in the alley behind her house and set it ablaze. She went to bed that night pleased with the day's work, the pleasant odor of Inquisition fresh in her nostrils.

As for me, I couldn't sleep for worrying about whether I would be the sacrificial lamb at our next monthly meeting for business.

I tossed and turned for two hours, then got dressed, put on my coat, and went for a walk. I headed toward town, past Grant's Hardware and the Legal Grounds, then turned west and passed by Kivett's Five and Dime. It was quiet outside. The houses were dark. I stopped for a moment and watched the fish tank in the front window of the barbershop, then walked past the Dairy Queen, now shuttered for the winter. Oscar and Livinia had left for Florida the week before.

There was a light on in the meetinghouse. I tried to remember if there had been a committee meeting that night and someone had left the lights on, a not uncommon occurrence. The back door was unlocked, which wasn't unusual, since Frank forgets to lock it half the time. I walked through the meeting room toward the office, when I heard a quick shuffle of feet and muffled whispering. Burglars! Probably poised to leap from a closet and shoot me down like a dog.

I backed out of the meetinghouse and jogged home the three blocks to call Bernie the policeman, who was asleep and had to get dressed and brush his teeth before meeting me back at the meetinghouse. It took him thirty minutes, and by that time whoever was in the church had left. One of my desk drawers was open, though nothing appeared to be missing.

I have several magazines hidden in my file cabinet under the letter *P* for *Progressive Christianity,* which I don't want anyone to know I read, for fear of being branded a godless heretic. Thankfully, they hadn't been discovered.

Bernie sniffed around the church a few minutes, poking his head into closets and shining his flashlight behind the furnace and into the crawl space beneath the cloakroom.

"Looks like whoever was here is gone," Bernie said. "You sure you heard someone?"

"Yes, there were at least two of them."

"Robbing a church," Bernie said, clearly disgusted. "People like that, they're goin' straight to Hades. Do not pass go, do not collect two hundred dollars."

"Well, it wasn't quite a robbery. It doesn't look like anything's missing."

"How about I loan you my gun. If they come back, you go ahead and plug 'em. Just make sure they're inside the church when you shoot 'em, so's we can call it self-defense."

"That's all right, Bernie, but I'd just as soon not kill anyone. It was probably just some kids. I'm sure everything will be fine."

He drove me home, and I fell into bed exhausted and slept until six o'clock the next morning when my boys began jumping on the bed. It was Saturday. I ate breakfast, then walked to the meetinghouse to finish my sermon. As I neared the meetinghouse, I heard the squeal of tires and saw a white car speed away with two people hunched down in the front seat. The license plate was smeared with mud.

Someone had been in my office. The file cabinets were open. A copy of *Progressive Christianity* lay open on the floor to the centerfold of Charles Darwin. Someone had drawn horns coming out of his head. Still, nothing seemed to be missing, so I didn't phone Bernie. Instead, I finished my sermon, then went home to spend the day with my family.

A little after midnight that night the phone rang. This isn't unusual for a pastor. I routinely field phone calls at all hours of the night from people who believe I'm wide awake, poised by the phone, waiting to solve their latest dilemma. Dale Hinshaw is particularly notorious for late-night calls, phoning to correct my thinking or elder me for some slight sin I had inadvertently committed.

So when the phone rang, I thought it was Dale and didn't pick it up. It rang a dozen times before falling silent. Five minutes later, there was a knock on the door. I pulled on my bathrobe and negotiated my way through the dark to the front door. It was Bernie.

"Got a light on down at the church and the back door's wide open. Thought you might want to catch 'em in the act."

I hurried upstairs, got dressed, and two minutes later was seated in Bernie's patrol car, as we eased our way through the ally in back of the meetinghouse. He slowed to a stop behind a white car.

"That car was here this morning," I said. "They must have come back."

Bernie unbuckled the flap over his pistol. This alarmed me greatly. The last time Bernie had unholstered his weapon, Bill Muldock had nearly been killed for taking a whiz in his own backyard in the middle of the night.

We left the car and crept across the parking lot, making our way toward the back steps of the meetinghouse, then up them and in. The light in my office was on and we could hear two people bickering. It sounded like women.

"It's not here, I tell you."

"Well, don't get mad at me. It was your idea, after all. I can't believe you didn't read it first."

I heard weeping and sniffling. "I knew you'd end up blaming it on me."

Then, in an exasperated tone, "Oh, quit your crying and help me look for it. Did you check Frank's desk?"

Bernie and I froze. At the moment, we were crouched behind Frank's desk. The door to my office opened and one of the Finchum daughters, the heavy one, appeared in the doorway.

"Freeze!" cried Bernie, leaping to his feet, his pistol extended.

The lights in the office went out and the electric pencil sharpener I kept on my desk came hurtling through the air, catching Bernie squarely in the face, though not before he'd managed to squeeze off a shot in the general direction of my office.

There were screams, the scent of gunpowder stung my nostrils, and my ears were ringing. Bernie slumped to the floor with a groan, done in by a pencil sharpener.

"We surrender," the Finchum daughters yelled, emerging from the office. They saw Bernie lying on the floor, out cold, blood dripping from his nose. "My Lord, we killed him," they cried in unison. The Finchum daughters did everything in unison and always had, as doing things together spared them the difficulty of having to think for themselves. They'd married the same day, to brothers, lived next door to one another, went to the same church—the Harmony Worship Center—and believed everyone who didn't share their narrow ideology was destined to spend eternity in a warm climate.

After a few minutes, Bernie began to stir, then moan. We helped him up to his feet and seated him in Frank's chair. An egg-shaped bump was rising on his forehead. He was still dazed, but after a moment his eyes began to focus on me. "Did I get 'em?"

"It appears you've killed my office clock," I informed him. "Fortunately, the Finchum daughters are alive and well."

He shook his head in confusion. "The Finchum daughters? What are they doing here?"

I turned to face them. "Yes, what are you doing here?"

They looked away.

"And you were here earlier, weren't you? Last night, and then again this morning?"

The heavy one was the first to speak. "You should be ashamed of yourself, reading magazines like *Progressive Christianity.*"

"Aha! So you're the one who drew the horns on Charles Darwin!" I had them dead to rights.

"Oh, just tell him," the other one said. "Then we can get it and get out of here."

"Tell me what?"

"It's that book we donated to your church in my father's name. We want it back. It's, uh, not appropriate for a church."

"Why didn't you just ask me for it?"

"We didn't want to be a bother."

"So, instead, you broke into the church, kept me up two nights in a row, and nearly killed Bernie with a pencil sharpener. This is your idea of not being a bother?"

"Maybe we went about it the wrong way," they conceded.

"Yes, maybe you did." Then I told them I didn't have the book, that I wasn't sure who did, but when I found it, I'd give them a call.

It had been a while since Bernie had arrested anyone. He was all for slapping the cuffs on the Finchum daughters and driving them to the jail in Cartersburg, but I managed to talk him out of it, pointing out that it wouldn't do wonders for his reputation to be known as the first police officer in history to lose a gun battle to a pencil sharpener.

We reached a compromise. I agreed not to press charges if they agreed not to tell anyone about my reading *Progressive Christianity*. They apologized to Bernie for knocking him out, and he apologized for trying to kill them. I was out an office clock, but decided not to push the issue.

Bernie was still dazed, so I drove him home in the patrol car, then walked the half dozen blocks to my house. Walking the streets at night was becoming a maddeningly familiar practice and one that was leaving me fairly tired.

The next morning, during meeting for worship, Hester Gladden stood and with obvious glee told how she'd burned the book, describing in delicious detail the curl of flames and the great plumes of smoke, which, she theorized, was not unlike hell, which was where the author of the book was headed, along with anyone who read it.

I sat in my chair behind the pulpit, reflecting on the sad state of theological education in the meeting. My Sunday school class that morning had been dreadful. We'd drawn one of Dale's questions from the hat. He writes a dozen questions for every one of someone else's, so we invariably draw one of his.

This morning he'd asked whether those who believed in a pre-millennial rapture are really Christian. I'd made the mistake of asking him what he meant by the term *premillennial rapture*, which led to a fifty minute monologue on the end times. If I'd been a fox caught in a trap, I'd have chewed off my leg to get away.

The questions I've been thinking of putting in the hat are these: Why am I silent about such insanity? Why am I so passive in the face of this fundamentalist lunacy? Why do I sit and listen to this foolishness with a smile on my face, as if his ideas merit my thoughtful consideration? Those are the questions that have lately been consuming me.

Deena and Dr. Pierce have stopped coming to the class. Deena told me it was nothing personal; they just didn't see how starting their week with Dale Hinshaw was a benefit to their spiritual journey. The class had dwindled down to Stanley Farlow, Dale, and myself. If I weren't the pastor, I wouldn't be there.

Now Hester had taken up book burning. Hester Gladden, whom I've known all my life and remember as a pleasant woman, now stricken with this cancer of intolerance. Attendance at church has been dropping. The only people we attract are folks like Albert Finchum, people who are dying and know they won't have to attend very many Sundays.

Hester finished speaking and I rose to my feet, propelled by some unseen force that I now believe to have been the Holy Spirit.

"What in the world does this have to with Jesus?" I asked.

Although this wasn't the question I anticipated asking, it seemed to grab everyone's attention. Miriam Hodge smiled, Hester and Dale frowned, and Asa Peacock, who didn't realize it was a rhetorical question, said, "Nothin', as far as I can tell."

Then, having held my tongue for four long years, I found my backbone, looked directly toward Dale and Hester, and said, in as firm a voice as I could muster, "And I'm renewing my subscription to *Progressive Christianity.*"

And with that, I gathered up my Bible and strode from the meetinghouse, suspecting my days as a pastor were numbered, but feeling wonderfully alive nonetheless.

Eighteen

Sam's Revelation

$\mathcal{D}$ecember blew in on a snowstorm. It was supposed to have rained, but the temperature dropped and it snowed instead, twelve inches, catching everyone off guard, including the county highway department, which had sent all its workers home. The roads out in the country drifted shut, sealing the farmers off. The few men who made it to the Coffee Cup on Saturday morning tried to remember the last time this much snow had come so early. Bob Miles dug through the old *Herald*s and found it hadn't snowed this much this early since 1953, so he wrote a big article about it being a fifty-year snow. He also announced that my son Addison had won that year's snowfall contest, accurately predicting the first inch of snow would fall on the third of December, which was his birthday and the date he picks for everything to happen.

Church services were canceled, except for those at Harmony Worship Center, who said that in light of all the Lord had done for them, the least they could do was slog through a little snow to get to church. Harmony Worship Center, I'm discovering, is one of these churches that never loses an opportunity to remind the rest of us how virtuous they are.

Miriam Hodge phoned me on Saturday evening to ask whether we should cancel services. Uly Grant and I had spent much of the day shoveling the parking lot and sidewalks, only to have them covered again with fresh snow. It was like trying to clean the house while the children were still home.

I was all for skipping church, reasoning it would give people more time to forget my behavior from the week before when I'd left the church in a self-righteous snit, fed up with what was passing for the Christian faith these days.

"What are the roads like out there?" I asked.

"We're shut in."

"Why don't we go ahead and cancel, Miriam. I'd hate for someone to fall and break a hip. Let's just keep folks home."

"I agree."

We divided the congregational directory in half to make phone calls. I asked for N-Z, so I wouldn't have to tell Dale Hinshaw, who I was sure would question our commitment. "What do you mean we're canceling church? Don't you think maybe we oughta trust the Lord to get us there okay? Boy, I bet the Lord is looking down on us right now and this is just breaking His heart, that Christians these days will deny their faith over a few snowflakes!"

We slept in the next morning, then woke up and ate pancakes. The boys wanted to go sledding, so we went to the basement, dug out the sleds, waxed the runners, and then headed toward the park, to the hill above the basketball court. By then, the sun was out in force and the snow was starting to melt. By noon, patches of pavement were showing through the snow, and by suppertime it was forty degrees and the streets were clear.

After supper, I walked down to the meetinghouse to check on things. It was very quiet, the temperature had dipped, and there was an icy sheen on the streets, so I picked my way carefully, staying to the snow so I wouldn't slip.

I let myself in the back door and walked through the meeting-house, turning on lights as I went. I sat in the fifth row, on the right side, where I had sat with my parents and brother, Roger, in my growing-up years. Just behind Ellis and Miriam Hodge. I lifted a hymnal from the rack in front of me and thumbed through it, reading the words and singing a few songs to myself.

Then I set the hymnal aside and closed my eyes, letting my other senses take over. The feel of the worn pew cushions, the smell of the meeting room—a mix of library smell, Murphy's oil soap, and the little blue discs Asa Peacock had been hanging in the toilets for the past thirty years.

The first things I learned about God I learned in this place, and at such an early age they had embedded themselves in my mind, like a child's handprint in fresh cement. I'd since learned other things about God, but it was those early images that were the most firmly entrenched. The God of my childhood was a tribal God, the personal God of Harmony Friends Meeting, who busied Himself tending to our wants and concerns, most of them involving safe travel, gainful employment, good health, and, failing that, a quick, painless death in our sleep.

As a teenager, it occurred to me that praying for God to do things that could be achieved with a little common sense and initiative was a misuse of God's talent. Though Pastor Taylor had always encouraged us to stand during the silence to share our insights about God, this was one revelation I kept to myself, having discerned that most folks, once they've made up their minds about God, tend not to appreciate further enlightenment.

Growing up, I had other thoughts about God, none of which I felt led to share with anyone else for fear of upsetting people. Like why, if God were so loving, He hated Communists and anyone else we happened to be against. Or why, if God were all-powerful, He allowed Dr. Neely's little boy to die. Or why a God who cared for the sparrows sent a tornado to tear down Stanley Farlow's barns, destroy his crops, and have the bank seize his farm. But I never asked these things, preferring instead to toe the party line and have the Friendly Women tell my mother what a fine young man I was.

Unfortunately, once you get in the habit of forsaking your convictions in order to be liked, it's hard to stop. I still catch myself nodding my head in agreement to things I haven't believed in years, then later despising myself for my cowardice.

Before I became a minister, I thought the hardest part would be writing a sermon every week. And at first it was, but then I built up a sufficient arsenal of clichés I could string together in a few hours' time and deliver something that seemed profound. The hardest part, I was learning, was telling the truth, when telling the truth meant losing your job, uprooting your family and moving them two states away to a church that hadn't heard of you. It added a whole new meaning to the biblical proverb that the truth would set you free.

I heard the creak of the front door and turned as Miriam Hodge walked in, stamping her feet clean on the floor mat.

I called out a greeting and asked what brought her into town.

"I'm on a milk run," she said. "I drove by and thought someone had left the lights on."

"Nope, just me."

"Well, sorry to disturb you, Sam. I'll let you be."

"No, that's fine. I was just woolgathering. Come on in."

She shrugged off her coat, hung it on a peg in the vestibule, and came and sat beside me. "So what is it that causes our pastor to be sitting in the meetinghouse all by himself at eight o'clock on a Sunday evening?"

I smiled. "Oh, just the usual things."

She looked at me, a mix of curiosity and sympathy on her face. "I've been worried about you, Sam."

"How come?"

"Well, I've known you all your life and I can't ever recall you storming out of church."

"Is that what I did?"

"You tell me, Sam."

I thought for a moment, watching tiny rivers of water run off Miriam's boots and onto the hardwood floor. "Yes, maybe I did."

"So who are you upset with?"

"The usual suspects—Dale and Fern and Hester and every other narrow-minded kook in this town." I told her about the Finchum daughters breaking into the meetinghouse and Dale's thoughts on the premillennial rapture. "What's wrong with these people? Why can't they think?"

Miriam chuckled, then let out a brief sigh. "So you stormed out of church because you're mad at them?"

I don't recall that I had ever been exasperated with Miriam Hodge, but her questions were starting to irritate me. "Well, of course I'm upset with them. Who wouldn't be?"

"Has your annoyance changed anything?"

"What do you mean?"

"Well, Sam, do Dale and Fern and Hester appear to be changing their behavior in order to please you?"

"Not so I've noticed."

"Then being upset with them isn't working, is it, Sam?"

"I suppose not."

We sat quietly, listening to the steady ticking of the Frieda Hampton memorial clock.

"I don't want to hurt your feelings," Miriam said after a bit, "but could I make a suggestion?"

"Sure."

"Why don't you stop trying to change them and work on changing yourself instead?"

"I'm not the one with the problem" I said, slightly peeved.

"Sam, how old are you now?"

"Forty-two."

"Don't you think it's time you started being the person God created you to be?"

"What do you mean?"

"I mean it's not working, Sam," she said, pointing to the pulpit. "You stand up there and say things you don't believe, just to make certain people happy, people who will never be happy anyway. Why not, instead of hiding your beliefs from everyone, just be who you are?"

"It isn't that easy," I said. "I could lose my job."

"Sam, you know what I think? I don't think you were mad at Dale and Fern and Hester last Sunday. I think you were mad at yourself. I think you're ashamed that you've spent sixteen years in ministry kowtowing to everybody and his brother and caving in and never taking a stand on anything important." She stomped her foot. "Grow up, Sam. Stop your whining and stop walking around like you're the only one with a burden. Give up the illusion that everyone is going to like you and just grow up." With that, Miriam Hodge rose from the pew and walked toward the front door. "Oh, and yes, Sam, I'm glad we had this little talk. Please give Barbara my love." And then she left.

If, when I had awakened that morning, someone had asked me how I believed my day would unfold, getting chewed out by Miriam Hodge would have been the last thing on my list.

I wanted to chase after Miriam and tell her she was mistaken, but inwardly I knew she wasn't, so I remained seated, angry and ashamed of myself. I was angry for having surrendered to spiritual mediocrity, for neglecting my obligation to speak the truth, inso-far as I understood it, and ashamed for caring too much what others thought of me and too little about what God might think.

I forced myself to reflect on Miriam's words in spite of their sting. It was not the kind of sting I felt when Dale rebuked me for failing to toe some arbitrary religious line, but a rarer sting— the one I felt when the lash of truth ripped my soul. And in those moments, the fifth pew became for me a seat of revelation: I had forsaken the gospel. Not Dale's gospel, miserly in its appli-cation, rigidly defining whom God loved and whom God didn't. That kind of gospel merited forsaking, and it was time I said so.

No, the gospel I'd forsaken was the one that served notice to the world, that refused to stay silent when people were crushed down and robbed of dignity and hope. I had learned about this gospel in seminary, but had abandoned it at the first sign of resistance, back in my first church, sixteen years ago. Now I was paying the price in self-contempt.

"Starting now," I promised God, "it's full steam ahead." I said it out loud, so God could hold me to it. "But Lord, if I get fired, You'll have to provide for my family." I said that out loud too, so I could hold God to it.

And sitting there, in the fifth pew, I was baptized. Not the dunk-in-the-water kind of baptism, but the sense that I was immersed in God's presence. A deep peace flooded over me, a calm assurance that all would be well, that the Dales of the world would not prevail.

"Lord, fill me Your truth and grace," I prayed. "And help me not be a jerk about it."

Then I rose to my feet, my loins girded for battle, ignorance and apathy my enemies, grace and truth my arms.

Nineteen

Dolores Makes a Break

The month of December sped past. To my deep disappointment, Christmas came and went without a hitch. I had been hankering for the opportunity to be more bold and to speak out against ignorance wherever I found it. Unfortunately, Dale chose that month to be perfectly appropriate. He made no mention of reviving his annual progressive Nativity scene. He didn't stand the Sunday before Christmas and ask people to raise their hands if they believed in the Virgin Birth. He didn't declare that Santa was the Antichrist, that if you moved three letters around *Santa* spelled *Satan*.

In fact, he had been unusually subdued the past several months. He had scaled down his salvation balloons ministry, cutting back the launches to once a month. Where he had once released hundreds of salvation balloons at a time, preferably when the wind would carry them toward Episcopalian strongholds, he now limited himself to a few dozen balloons and didn't seem to care where they landed. He offered no explanation except that being around all that helium made him talk funny, but I suspect that was just an excuse.

In the weeks before Christmas, he was curiously reserved during Sunday school. He stopped loading the hat with questions and for the first Sunday in memory didn't bring his chart showing the time line for the Lord's return.

I worried he might be dying, but the more I thought about it, the more unlikely it seemed. Dale isn't the type to slip quietly into the night. If he were dying, he'd want everyone to know. He would encourage everyone to reflect on the frailty of life and urge them to be saved, even though we've all been saved three or four times. He would boast about fighting the good fight and finishing the race and keeping the faith, how he was looking forward to the crown of righteousness. He would make his death the focus of our church, so that when he died we would be secretly relieved.

When New Year's passed and he remained unusually passive, I went to visit him. I didn't call first, which I usually do. I was driving past, saw Dale's car in their driveway, and on a whim pulled in behind it. In the four years I'd been their pastor, I'd never visited the Hinshaws. Seeing Dale at church was enough fellowship for me; I didn't crave more.

A variety of concrete animals were arrayed across their front yard, along with a wishing well, a windmill, and a plywood cutout of a man leaning against a tree fishing with the phrase "*I will make you fishers of men*" painted down one leg.

I rang the doorbell and from deep within the bowels of their home I could hear the faint strains of the Doxology. When I was a teenager, a man from the Good News Doorbell Company of Cedar Rapids, Iowa, had come through our town selling doorbells guaranteed to inspire the saints and convict the wayward of their sins.

The speaker for our annual revival had fallen ill when the doorbell salesman happened along, which the elders at Harmony Friends interpreted as a sign from God, so they invited him to preach our revival. He spoke about the thousands of people added to the Kingdom through the ministry of the Good News doorbells. He read several stirring testimonials, one from a Fuller Brush salesman trapped in a life of sin, who happened to ring a Good News doorbell, hear "Just as I Am," think of his sainted mother, break down in tears, give his heart to the Lord, and become a missionary serving in Africa among the headhunters. It was a stirring account, leaving grown men reaching for their handkerchiefs.

In addition to the Doxology, extra doorbell hymns could be purchased each month, with appropriate hymns for Christmas, Easter, and the Fourth of July. Dale had bought the entire set, which had resulted in children all over town ringing his doorbell each month so they could hear the tunes. Several of the children made up alternative lyrics that were less than godly, driving Dale to distraction. He would charge out of his house and try to catch them, but I always got away. I was young and nimble and, though he says he's forgiven me, I sometimes wonder.

Now the only hymn that still played was the Doxology, Dale's least favorite hymn because it smacks of Catholicism. It ran through two verses before he opened the door. He hadn't shaved that morning, wore wrinkled clothes, and was bleary-eyed. He looked like Uly Grant's father used to look after an evening at the Buckhorn bar.

His appearance so startled me, my pastoral tact deserted me. "What's wrong, Dale? You look terrible."

His grizzled chin began to tremble. "It's Dolores. She left me."

"She what?"

"She left me. I woke up this morning and there was a note on the table and her suitcase is gone. Her sister came and got her."

"Just to visit though, right? She didn't *leave-you* leave you, did she?"

Dale nodded his head miserably, then began to weep.

My pastoral instincts kicked in. I put my arm around him, steered him into the living room to the couch, then sat down beside him. "Dale, let's start at the beginning."

"She's been real mad at me. I gave our anniversary money to the Mighty Men of God and then I burned the car, and now she's sayin' she's made a New Year's resolution to leave me."

I sat quietly, not knowing what to say. Dale continued to cry with phlegmy heaves and occasional snorts, pausing occasionally to wipe his nose on his shirt sleeve. I edged closer to him and patted his back. "Look on the bright side, Dale. People never keep their New Year's resolutions. She'll be back before you know it."

But she didn't return that day, or the next. I stopped by Dale's house each morning to fix his breakfast and encourage him along, but it wasn't helping. He'd gone three days without shaving and hadn't changed his clothes. He looked as if he'd been shipwrecked and washed up on the shore. He wasn't eating, except for the tiny bit of scrambled eggs I forced upon him each morning.

On the third day, at Dale's request, I phoned Dolores at her sister's house in the city and urged her to return, which she refused to do. "It's been like this forty-one years, Sam. He thinks only of himself, and I'm worn out. It took me ten years to save that money for our anniversary cruise, and he gave it away without even askin' me. I'm fed up." Then she hung up the phone.

"What'd she say?" Dale asked. "Is she comin' home?"

"Probably not anytime soon," I said. "Dale, we need to talk."

I tried to think what I could tell him without violating pastoral confidentiality. "I have the feeling Dolores is very upset with you. Do you understand why she might feel that way?"

He nodded his head glumly. "She's real mad about me givin' away our cruise money." He let out a sob and wiped his nose on his sleeve, which, after three days of wiping, was rather unsightly. My stomach rolled.

I decided to postpone our conversation and get him cleaned up. "But first things first," I said, helping him to his feet. "Let's get you in the shower and get some fresh clothes on you." I helped him to the bathroom, turned on the water for a shower, then went to his bedroom, pulled a clean shirt and a pair of pants from their hangers and laid them on the bathroom countertop.

"Okay, Dale, you take your shower and go ahead and shave and put on these clean clothes. And don't forget to change your underwear. Trust me, you'll feel 100 percent better."

I let myself out, then went to my office, and phoned Dolores again, pleading with her to return. "He's really going downhill," I told her. "He needs you."

"I can't talk now," she said. "My sister and I are getting massages today. I might call you later, but don't wait up."

Three days away from her husband and she's already letting some stranger rub his paws all over her, I thought. I was learning loads about Dolores Hinshaw, not all of it good.

Then she hung up again, something I was getting used to.

I sat at my desk, pondering what the extent of my involvement in the Hinshaw marriage should be. Counseling wasn't my strong suit, and the idea of spending quality time with Dale wasn't all that appealing.

I stopped by each day that week to check on Dale. He wasn't doing any better. Uninterested in all hobbies and activities, he confided that he hadn't launched a salvation balloon the entire week. "I've lost my heart for the lost," he said. "I just sit around and think about Dolores."

"She'll be back," I assured him, though I wasn't persuaded myself. "She just needed some time away."

He came to church by himself that Sunday. He slipped in after the start of worship and left before it ended. He sat slumped in his pew, defeated and worn, a broken man.

My phone rang early the next day. "How's Dale?" It took me a moment to figure out who was asking.

"Dolores, perhaps you should call him and ask him yourself. I'm sure he'd be happy to hear from you."

"Can't today," she said. "My sister and I are going to Louisville."

"What's in Louisville?"

"The riverboat casino," she said. "I had a hundred dollars left in our cruise fund and it's burning a hole in my pocket."

She was out of control.

Ironically, scarcely a week after I'd worked up the courage to voice my liberality, I found myself reverting to the theology of my childhood. "Dolores, as your pastor, I must say that you're on spiritually shaky ground. You need to come home to your husband."

"Don't be such a wet blanket, Sam. It's time I lived a little. By the way, if you see Dale, remind him to water the houseplants." Then she hung up the phone on me, again.

I got dressed, ate breakfast, then went past Dale's house. He was still in bed. The doorbell played through four verses before he opened the door. He had slept in his clothes.

I steered him toward the bathroom, turned on the shower, and laid out fresh clothes. While he was getting dressed, I fixed his breakfast: scrambled eggs, toast with butter and strawberry jam (butter first, then jam—he was getting pickier every day), bacon (not quite crisp, but not chewy either), and coffee.

By now his appetite had recovered and he tapped his coffee

cup against the edge the table in rapid succession when he wanted it refilled. It was all I could do not to break it over his head. "Don't forget the cream," he said.

"Dolores phoned this morning," I said.

"She did! Is she comin' home today?"

"No, not today. She and her sister are going to Louisville for a boat ride."

"In the middle of winter?"

"Apparently so. Anyway, she wanted you to water the house-plants."

"Gee, Sam, could you do that for me? I just don't have it in me right now."

"Sure, Dale."

There were a lot of plants. It took me fifteen minutes to water them, then another twenty minutes to wash the breakfast dishes.

"Do you know how to run a washing machine?" Dale asked, as I wiped the counter dry.

"Sure."

"Maybe you could start a load of laundry. I'm running out of skivvies."

"I can show you how to run it, Dale. It's not hard."

"It's those basement stairs," he said. "I can't get up and down 'em very easy on these old knees." He chuckled. "Guess I've worn 'em out praying on 'em all these years." Vintage Dale, taking every opportunity to remind me of his piety.

"Tell you what, Dale, why don't you gather up your underwear and I'll get them started."

I started the washer, then prepared to leave. "I'll be back later today to move them to the dryer."

"What's for lunch?" he asked.

"How about the Coffee Cup?"

"Can't afford it," he said. "They're wanting three-fifty for the hamburger platter now. Must think people in this town are made of money."

I reached into my wallet and pulled out a twenty. "This'll get you through the week, Dale."

"What about my pie?"

"What pie?"

"The pie I like to eat with my hamburger platter."

...a ten-dollar bill and handed it over.

"Thanks, Sam."

"No problem, Dale."

"Sure am gonna be awful thirsty, though."

"Why's that?"

"Coffee's a dollar a cup now."

I handed him a five, which was the last of my money.

"How about tip money? I'd hate for Heather to think I'm cheap."

"Check your couch cushions."

It took me an hour to track down an address for Dolores's sister, and another two hours to drive to the city. I sat for four hours in her driveway until they arrived home from the riverboat.

"What are you doing here, Sam?"

"I've come to take you home, Dolores."

"Is Dale at the end of his rope?"

"No, I am. Now please get your suitcase and come with me."

"Sam, you don't know what it's like to live with that man."

"I'm starting to get an idea, and I am not without sympathy. But you've made your point, and we'll make Dale promise to go to marriage counseling if you come home. I think he'll agree to that now."

"You think?"

"If he doesn't, I'll kill him. Either way, your problem will be solved."

I had her home in time for supper. As we turned into the driveway, she began to tear up, and when Dale came to the door, they broke down.

I arranged them in a sodden lump on the couch. "You," I said, pointing to Dale, "will attend marriage counseling with your wife. Is that understood?"

"Yes."

"And you," I said, singling out Dolores, "will stop being a doormat and stop running away from home and gambling and letting strangers massage you. Is that clear?"

She sniffed and nodded her agreement.

"I'm going home now. I'll meet with you tomorrow, and we'll make arrangements for marriage counseling."

"Sam, before you leave, could you switch my underwear to the dryer like you promised?" Dale asked.

It was going to be a long winter. I could tell that now. And if I made it through without violating my commitment to nonviolence, it would be a miracle.

Twenty

Our Winter Meditations

The weather broke at the end of January. It had been a cold winter with heavy snow, the schools had closed four times, and parents all over town were deep in prayer that the weather would improve, which it finally did. Ned Kivett at the Five and Dime was so desperate for warm weather, he set up his annual bathing suit display a month early. He dressed his new mannequin in a bikini and propped her up in the front window, causing no small amount of scandal among certain townspeople.

It was the first bikini to ever appear in the window of the Five and Dime. Before this, Ned had only sold one-piece bathing suits that covered everything but the wrists and ankles. He had received the bikini by mistake. At first he thought it was a pair of ear muffs and an eye patch, though a closer look revealed it was, in fact, a bikini, and not a very large one at that. If the weather hadn't been so bad, he would have returned it. But the cold weather and the gray days have weakened his moral defenses, so he put it on the mannequin instead.

While the Friendly Women were busy circulating petitions demanding Ned cease and desist, the men at the Coffee Cup began speculating about who might purchase the bikini. After much deliberation, it was decided only three women in town could actually wear the bikini and do it justice—Heather Darnell at the Coffee Cup, the recently dethroned Sausage Queen, Tiffany Nagle, and Deena Morrison.

Bets were placed as to which of the three would eventually purchase it. The smart money was on Tiffany Nagle, so you can imagine our surprise when Dr. Pierce waltzed into the Five and Dime on a Wednesday afternoon, plunked down twenty dollars, and waited while Ned undressed the mannequin, packed the bikini in a plain brown wrapper, and handed it over to Dr. Pierce, blushing all the while.

This led to all sorts of theories about Dr. Pierce among the Coffee Cup crowd, none of them complimentary, until Asa Peacock pointed out he probably bought it for Deena, his bride-to-be. "Probably for their honeymoon," Asa said.

"That's gonna be some honeymoon," Kyle Weathers observed, with more than a touch of envy.

The Coffee Cup fell silent as the men contemplated Deena's honeymon.

"So has anyone heard where they're going?" I asked, feeling it my duty as a minister to shift the focus of their attention away from Deena and her bikini.

"Someplace warm, I'd guess, with a bikini like that," Bob Miles said.

"Where'd you and Barbara go, Sam?" Asa asked.

"Cincinnati, to see the Reds play."

"That's some wife you got there," Vinny Toricelli said. The other men nodded their agreement.

"Me and Jessie went to Peoria to visit her aunt," Asa said. "I think about it every time I hear our song."

"What's your song?" I asked.

"'Moonlight Over Peoria.' Do you know it?"

"I don't believe so."

"It didn't get a lot of play time around here," Asa conceded.

We discussed other trips we'd taken, being careful not to sound too enthusiastic. Travel is viewed with suspicion in our town, as it implies a dissatisfaction with staying home. Travel to the neighboring states is fine, so long as one doesn't make a habit of it and is quick to declare that, although it was a fine place to visit, they wouldn't want to live there. In 1971, Harvey and Eunice Muldock visited Puerto Rico and came back with pictures. People still talk about it, and not charitably.

As for honeymoons, they are opportunities to visit relatives you haven't seen for a while, so spouses can know what it is they've gotten themselves into.

Travel to Europe is acceptable, but only in the event of war, to put down the occasional fascist uprising. Otherwise, it's pretentious and people will think you're a snob. Dr. Neely and his wife visited France this past August. The trip was a gift from their daughters, so they had to go. But they did the right thing and told everyone they had a miserable time, were glad to be home, and if they never went back it wouldn't be too soon. People have been willing to forgive them, because if they hadn't gone, then Dr. Pierce would never have come to town and he and Deena wouldn't have met. So it was God's will that Dr. Neely and his wife went to France. Yet one more example of God bringing something good from tragedy and hardship.

The trustees at the church have been painting the inside of the meetinghouse, on the assumption Deena will be getting married there. She had told me she might be married in the city, where she grew up, though I haven't told anyone, for fear the trustees will lose their motivation for sprucing up the meetinghouse. I encourage them each afternoon by mentioning how grateful Deena is for their thoughtfulness, then suggesting that while they're at it they might as well replace the carpet.

The carpet was installed thirty years ago. It was donated by the late Esther Farlow, who knew six months in advance she was going to die and used that time traveling from one carpet store to another before finding the carpet she wanted—an utterly repulsive lime green shag. Esther, I now suspect, was passive-aggressive and wanted to annoy us in perpetuity, knowing once a church has installed carpet it takes an act of God to get it removed.

To my utter amazement, the trustees let loose of ten thousand dollars and had new carpeting installed. They sought no one's counsel but their own. They simply ripped out the old carpet and replaced it, figuring it would be easier to apologize than to ask permission.

The carpet is a muted gray, the meetinghouse walls a soft blue with white trim. It is a vast improvement, well worth the headache I received from the paint fumes. I've been spending a lot of time in the back booth of the Coffee Cup, writing my sermons there until the fumes dissipate and I can return to my office. Though I might not go back. It has been a pleasant experience. Heather keeps my glass of iced tea full, and Vinny lets me eat all the day-old pie I want.

The restaurant patrons have been diligent in providing me a variety of illustrations and ideas for my sermon. They tell bawdy jokes about traveling salesmen and farmers' daughters, then grant me permission to use them in my messages. That sets off a round of chortles and snickers. They seem to delight at the opportunity to lead me astray.

"You hang around here long enough, and we'll expand your vocabulary," Vinny promised. "You ministers spend all your time with little old ladies. You need to get out more, like Jesus did. You never saw him hanging around with church people. He ate with sinners."

"Yes, and it got him killed," I pointed out.

I told Vinny if he wanted me to stay he'd have to install a phone jack at my booth so I could call people, and three days later, there it was, along with a sign: *The Harmony Friends Meeting Annex.* Some people spend their winters in Florida, which I can't do, given our town's feelings about travel. So I'm spending my winter at the Coffee Cup, in the warm fellowship of sinners.

There are benefits I didn't anticipate, which make my time here all the more pleasant. Fern Hampton won't come near the place, citing the moral depravity of its patrons. In fact, they're quite virtuous. They just act depraved so people like Fern will keep their distance.

I've even been doing some counseling here. I've noticed people feel freer to stop by and visit, people who would never show up at my office and admit to having problems, but who will join me at the annex, sip on their coffee, and unburden themselves.

Dale and Dolores Hinshaw have been stopping by. After their brief separation, I'd met with them twice and suggested to Dale that he might spend less time saving the lost and more time with his wife, so he's been bringing her to the Coffee Cup for lunch. Though that isn't quite what I had in mind, it seems to be working. She told me it had been two weeks since she'd had the urge to choke him.

If they hadn't been married so long, I'd be worried about them. But there is, I'm discovering, an inertia inherent in some long-term marriages that makes parting difficult. Divorce would require opening new checking accounts and cleaning out the basement, which, when you're past fifty, strikes some people as too much work. So they put up with one another and maybe hope that God in His mercy might call their spouse home and grant them freedom.

Couples who should never have married in the first place stay together sixty or seventy years so the dreadful task of cleaning their basement will fall to someone else, namely, their children. My parents get along well, though I live in mortal fear they will stay in their home until their deaths, leaving me to deal with the staggering accumulation of their union. For years, I have urged them to have a garage sale, which they've refused to do. Now my only hope is that they will divorce and be forced to clean their own basement.

There was a woman in our town, years ago, named Myra Stapert, whose pack rat husband died, leaving her with a house full of junk, which she remedied by setting the place on fire and moving to an apartment over Grant's Hardware. People rushed to assist her, giving her clothing, food, Tupperware, mismatched sets of dinnerware, and old television sets. Within three months, she was worse off than before, a victim of charity. Her only option was to leave town in the middle of the night. We never heard from her again.

I shudder to think what Deena and Dr. Pierce's children will think when they happen upon her bikini fifty years from now, tucked away in a trunk up in the attic. Or maybe find an old, yellowed picture of their sainted mother standing on a beach dressed very simply. "Is that Mom? That looks like her, but that can't be her, can it? She wouldn't wear anything like that, would she?" I'm glad I won't be around to have to deal with the fallout.

Or when Dale and Dolores pass away and their oldest son, Raymond Dale, will clean out the top drawer of Dale's desk and find the letters he wrote to Dolores when she left him for a week. He'll recognize his father's spidery handwriting. "Why did you leave? Please come back. I promise I'll change. I'll get the money back. Please come home. I miss you. I need you." Letters Dale wrote, but never mailed. They're still there and soon he'll forget about them and one day, years from now, Raymond Dale will discover them and the image of his parents that has sustained him all these years will be shattered.

Myra Stapert had the right idea when she burned all the evidence.

When people came to church the last Sunday in January, they walked in, saw the new carpet, and had a fit. Why weren't they told? Had this been discussed? Did the trustees have the authority to do such a thing? Why gray? Why not red? For that matter, what was wrong with the old carpet? With all the starving children in the world, was it good stewardship to throw money away when we already had perfectly good carpet?

Fern Hampton demanded to see the bill of sale, so she could find out which trustee had the temerity to order new carpet without consulting her. But it couldn't be found. The trustees had the good sense to dispose of everything that would connect them to this heinous crime.

"I think it was Harvey Muldock's idea," Asa told Fern, who promptly stormed off to Harvey, only to be told it was Ellis Hodge, who admitted to nothing except to say he thought it was Dale's idea. Dale sent her to Stanley Farlow, who forwarded her to Bill Muldock, who told her he'd heard it was her idea.

It hasn't been an easy winter for Fern, having to oversee the town's morality when it seems bent on depravity. She stopped by the Five and Dime to harangue Ned Kivett for selling bikinis.

"What bikinis?" he asked. "I don't see any bikinis." He pointed to his mannequin, now attired in a floor-length gown. "Does that look like a bikini to you?"

He has ordered more bikinis, which he keeps behind the counter, out of children's view. He only sells them to people twenty-one and older, if they promise not to wear them inside the city limits.

The church elders postponed the January meeting because of the painting, so we met the first week of February instead. After we had waded through the committee reports, Miriam Hodge asked if there was any new business. With Dolores home, Dale has revived and happily announced he would be launching five hundred salvation balloons the next week, targeting the annual convention of Unitarians in the city. Miriam wanted to minute our appreciation to the trustees for sprucing up the meetinghouse, but Fern nipped that in the bud, then demanded we investigate rumors of financial improprieties concerning the trustees and their purchase of the carpet.

Winter, I'm starting to believe, gives us too much time to contemplate the world's evils—bikinis, world travel, new carpet, and Unitarians. Then again, we have to think about something, and it's always more fun to meditate on someone else's sin instead of our own.

Twenty-one

A Sudden Turn

*I*t's been two months since Miriam Hodge advised me to speak my mind. I've been looking for the opportunity, but no one has cooperated. I kept hoping Dale would do something stupid so I could take exception, but he'd been most compatible, going so far as to recommend the church give me a raise. Everyone has been unusually reasonable, except for Fern Hampton, and I wasn't about to stand up to her. Speaking my mind was one thing; suicide by Fern was another.

Dr. Pierce and Deena had returned to our Sunday school class, buoying my spirits. And several of the alumni from the Live Free or Die class had stopped attending, which was icing on the cake. The questions I pulled from the hat each Sunday were startling in their boldness, obviously written by someone who didn't know certain questions shouldn't be asked. It reminded me how often we in the church ask the same safe questions, give the same pat answers, and then applaud our intellectual vigor.

My first year of seminary, I met a man who'd retired from there years before. His wife had died and he had nowhere else to go, so he passed his days at the seminary where he'd taught. He set up residence in the student lounge and, in addition to teaching me Ping-Pong, enlightened me on a range of other topics.

I complained to him one day that my faith had died, how I mourned its passing, that I wasn't sure what to believe, and if it were up to me, I'd just as soon return to what I had once believed. He laughed, then asked if I had ever heard of Oliver Wendell Holmes Jr.

"Wasn't he in those old detective movies?"

"No, that was Sherlock Holmes. Oliver Wendell Holmes Jr. was on the Supreme Court."

"Oh," I said, wondering what a Supreme Court justice had to do with my problem.

"Holmes said that the mind, once expanded to the dimensions of larger ideas, never returns to its original size."

I thought about that for a moment.

"You've been stretched, Sam. Now you have to fill your mind with a grand vision. That's why you're here."

So that's what I did. I read and listened and cleaned the attic of my mind in order to make room for the new. I learned how to interpret the Bible, how to ask questions and think theologically. Unfortunately, I didn't learn that some churches don't appreciate grand visions, or higher biblical criticism, or theology, for that matter. Except, of course, the theology they grew up with and prefer to keep, lest new knowledge require a change of heart and mind.

In my first church, I was counseled to stick to the customary, not rock the boat, and above all not upset a certain Sunday school class, whose members hadn't had a new thought since 1962 and didn't want one. Eventually, I returned to the clichés of my childhood faith, put my theology books in storage, and made sure to visit the people in the nursing home. I kept that pattern the twelve years I pastored that church and fell into it again when I returned to Harmony. Sixteen years of letting my mind atrophy like a spent balloon, once stretched but now withered.

But lately I've been leaving church positively buoyant. It's such an odd sensation I wasn't sure what to make of it. I thought at first it was the cough medicine I'd been taking, which has a tendency to make me loopy-happy, but it finally occurred to me it was something else entirely, a feeling so foreign to me it took a while to name it. I was optimistic.

"What's wrong with you?" my wife asked on a Sunday evening in late February. The boys were in bed and we were sitting in front of the fireplace, watching the sparks jump. "You don't seem yourself lately. You seem, almost . . ." She paused to think of the word.

"Content?" I said.

"That's it," she agreed. "Content."

"Everything is going so well. I love our Sunday school class. I never dreamed we'd have a Sunday school class like this."

"It has been fun. Deena and Dr. Pierce are wonderful additions."

"For the first time, I feel I can invite people to church without being embarrassed," I said. "Even Dale has settled down."

My wife smiled and reached for my hand. "I'm glad things are going better, honey."

We stayed up another hour, reading and enjoying the fire, content beyond measure.

It has been said by old soldiers that it's the bullet you don't hear that kills you. My phone rang early the next morning, my day off. It was Bea Majors on a self-appointed inquisition.

"I heard Dr. Pierce said during Sunday school he didn't believe in the Virgin Birth of Jesus."

"I don't think he came right out and said it like that, Bea. Why don't you ask him?"

"I did. And do you know what he told me?"

"I haven't the faintest idea."

"He told me he'd learned a long time ago how babies were made."

"Bea, what would you like me to do about it? We don't kill heretics anymore. It's against the law."

"Well, I just want to say I've been playing the organ in this church for fifty years, and I'm not sure I can continue to play for a minister who doesn't believe in the Virgin Birth."

"I never said I didn't believe in the Virgin Birth. It's Dr. Pierce who doesn't believe in it."

"Oh, so you admit that he doesn't."

Now I was utterly confused. "No, I don't know that for sure. I just thought we were talking about him, not me."

"So how come all of a sudden you want to talk about Dr. Pierce and not yourself. Have you got something to hide, Sam?"

"Not at all, Bea."

"Then maybe you should tell me what you think of the Virgin Birth."

"I don't know what to think of it, quite frankly," I said.

"So you don't believe it either?"

"I didn't say that. I said I didn't know what to think of it."

"Sam, maybe you just need to find yourself a new organist. I think maybe I need to go somewhere else to church."

"Bea, why don't I come by your house and we talk. This seems awfully sudden."

Bea Majors was the worst organist in the Western world. Why I was talking her into staying was an even greater mystery to me than the Virgin Birth.

"No, Sam, I've made up my mind."

"Bea, I wish you'd reconsider."

"I don't think so," she said rather stiffly. "I've given it all the thought I need to. Good-bye."

I set the phone down, more than a little troubled.

It was too much to hope Bea would go quietly into the night. Instead, she began working the phones, notifying the rest of the congregation I didn't believe in the Virgin Birth and was probably, at that very moment, sacrificing firstborn children on the church altar.

By suppertime, I'd received half a dozen phone calls from members of the church demanding I explain myself. I held them off by saying, as firmly as I could, that I agreed with the Apostle Paul on the Virgin Birth. That seemed to satisfy them, though I knew if they discovered Paul never mentioned it, I'd be in trouble.

I wasn't too worried they would find that out. They're nice people, but not well versed in Scripture. Many of them have cherished proverbs that they attribute to the Bible.

"Well, you know what the Bible says about that, when the cat's away, the mice will play." Or "Like it says in the Bible, a hog in satin is still a hog."

I had stopped correcting them long ago, having learned that people who talk the most about the Bible often know it the least, but resent having it pointed out. So I cultivated the habit of nodding my head in agreement, as if marveling at their exegetical prowess.

But that didn't work this time. On Tuesday afternoon, Miriam Hodge stopped by the meetinghouse to tell me three people had phoned her demanding my resignation. Dale and Dolores, who just the week before had been my new best friends, joined forces against me. Although I was heartened to see them united for a common cause, I was somewhat distressed that their common cause was getting me fired.

"This is so silly," I said to Miriam. "I never said I didn't believe in the Virgin Birth. All I did was mention to Bea that I didn't know what to think of it. That's all I said."

"Sam, this is easily solved. The church newsletter comes out next week. Why don't you write on the pastor's page that you believe in the Virgin Birth? That ought to pacify them."

I sat quietly, considering her request. "Does this mean you weren't serious two months ago when you told me I needed to stop trying to make people happy who'll never be happy anyway?"

"Did I say that?"

"Yes. You also said I should stop kowtowing to everyone and I needed to give up the illusion everyone is going to like me."

"I said all those things?" Miriam asked.

"You also told me it was time I grew up."

"That was a bad day for me," Miriam said. "I'm going through the change right now and it's making me edgy."

"No need to apologize, Miriam. You were absolutely right."

I stood, walked around my desk to Miriam, put my arm around her shoulder, and walked her to the door. "I appreciate your advice, but I won't be writing anything in the newsletter. I'm not going to be held hostage by unreasonable people. I'm not sure what I think of the Virgin Birth. I do know I'm not going to say I believe it just to make people happy. If they don't like it, they can go somewhere else to church."

"Fair enough, Sam. But I don't think they want to go somewhere else. I think they want you to do the going."

"I'm willing to take that risk," I said. "I guess we're going to have to decide what kind of church we're going to be, whether we'll be rigid and hidebound or tolerant and generous in spirit."

"Yes, I suppose you're right, Sam. But I'm not looking forward to the discussion."

"You know, Miriam, it might turn out to be a blessing. We could end up deciding what's most important to us."

"I know that and you know that. What concerns me is that Dale and Bea will decide what's most important is to have you crucified."

I laughed. "At least I'd be in good company."

"That you would, Sam. That you would."

I thanked her for stopping past and hugged her good-bye.

I turned to walk into my office.

"You," Frank said, perched in his secretary's chair, peering at me over the top of his bifocals, "are a dead man walking."

"What do you mean?"

"I mean Dale has a bullet with your name on it. You are not long for this world. You're history. Yesterday's news. The word at the Coffee Cup this morning is that you'll be gone by Easter."

"Thank you, Frank. Your honesty is certainly an encouragement to me."

"Just keeping you informed, that's all."

"That's very kind of you."

"So how come you're denying the virginity of our Blessed Mother?" he asked.

"I've done no such thing. As far I'm concerned, she's a fine example of femininity and if I had a daughter, I'd name her Mary. I'm just tired of a few nutty people getting worked up over nothing."

"Oh, so now you think the Virgin Mary is nothing."

"You know, I could find a new secretary if I had to. One who treats me with a little more respect and doesn't twist my words."

Frank smiled, then leaned back in his chair. "Who'd want this job? The pay's lousy and you have to put up with crazy people. I'm only sticking around to see how you get out of this."

"Your loyalty is touching, Frank."

"Well, Sam, you go about your business stirring up trouble, and I'll watch your backside. Even though it's not in my job description and I haven't gotten a raise in three years."

"If I survive this, I'll ask the elders to do something about that."

"That's all right. It'd probably just kick me into a higher tax bracket.

Besides, I'm hoping the Lord will let me slip into heaven on your coattails." He paused for a moment. "Course now that you've insulted his mother, those coattails probably aren't nearly as long."

He walked from the office, twitching with laughter.

I returned to my desk to start work on my sermon. The phone rang. I wasn't in the mood to be rebuked, so I let the answering machine pick it up. It was my superintendent up in the city, calling to see if what he'd heard from Bea Majors was true, that I had stood in the pulpit and called the Virgin Mary a floozy.

He'd be driving down to Harmony next week, he said, to meet with the elders and me. He went on, his voice cold and mechanical through the answering machine speaker. "I'll expect you to say that Mary was a virgin. If you don't, I'll have to recommend they let you go." A sharp click followed, then the room fell silent.

That's when I realized this wasn't going to go away, that my critics had marshaled their forces, and I was soon going to be out the door.

Twenty-two

The Last Stand

Bea Majors self-imposed exile lasted one week. She was back the next Sunday, poised at the organ, hanging on my every word, ready to drown out any perceived sacrilege with a burst of hymns. A tape recorder sat on the organ, its twin wheels turning silently, gathering proof of my blasphemy.

I didn't speak with her at first, hoping to avoid any unpleasantries, but after worship I thought better of it and approached her. She was standing in a knot of people occasionally pointing in my direction. When I walked over to her, most of them scattered like chickens.

"Don't try to talk me into staying, Sam Gardner. I just came today to get my music. You're in big trouble with the superintendent."

"I wish you hadn't phoned him, Bea."

"I bet you do. There's nothing like having a little light cast on your dark deeds."

"Bea, I never made any disparaging comments about the Virgin Mary from the pulpit. You're telling lies about me, and you need to stop. It's hurtful to my reputation and bad for the church."

213

Her chin began to tremble, and she began to weep. People edged closer, staring. Bea's sister, Opal, pointed her finger in my face. "Shame on you, Sam. Attacking an old woman until she cries. You ought to be ashamed of yourself."

"Sam's not done anything," Miriam Hodge said. "And he's absolutely right. Bea has been spreading rumors about him, and it needs to stop. Right now."

Fern Hampton waded into the fray. "Well, I never thought I'd live to see the day when we'd let someone come between us Friendly Women."

"That isn't the point, Fern," Miriam said. "Bea is causing trouble, and it's time we said so. You're an elder in this church, just like me. We have a responsibility to help hold people accountable. It's time we did our job."

I was going to intervene, but recalled advice my father had given me years before. "Son," he'd said, "don't ever get between two women in a fight. They'll scratch your eyes out. Just get away as quick as you can."

So that is what I did.

Miriam phoned me later that day. "Thanks for sticking around, Sam. Your bravery is an inspiration."

"Sorry, Miriam. I just wasn't ready for that."

"You'd better get ready. I have a feeling it's going to get a lot worse. Fern and Dale have asked me to call a special meeting of the elders."

"Are you going to do it?"

"If two elders ask for it, we have to do it."

I groaned at the thought.

"The thing is, Sam, they want to have it this Tuesday while the superintendent's here, and I can't be there. That's the night of the science fair and Amanda's getting an award. I think they knew that. Fern's the assistant clerk, so she'll be in charge. You're going to have to face them on your own."

"How about Asa Peacock? Will he be there?"

"No, he and Jessie are out of town visiting their son. Won't be back until Friday."

"How about Harvey Muldock?"

"He has an Odd Fellows meeting that night."

The situation was looking grim.

"Don't worry, Sam. They can't fire you without the church's approval. Just go and let them vent their spleens and everything will turn out fine."

I took the next day off, then spent Tuesday barricaded in my office with Frank guarding the door. At supper, despite an overwhelming desire to vomit, I choked down a sandwich at the urging of my wife.

I arrived at the meetinghouse just in time for the meeting. Dale, Fern, Opal, and the superintendent were arrayed around the folding table down in the basement. Dale began the meeting with a prayer. It turned quickly into an editorial against modernity in general and scientific discovery in particular, which caused certain so-called Christians to abandon the truth of Scripture and fall into depravity.

"Well," Fern said, when Dale finished praying, "I think we all know why we're here. Sam's gone off the deep end again. Two years ago he didn't believe in God and now he's denying the Virgin Birth."

"Don't forget what he did last year," Dale said. "Had Deena Morrison preach on sexual perversion the Sunday before Christmas."

Opal shook her head in disgust.

"What have you got to say for yourself, Sam?" the superintendent asked.

I wasn't sure what to say for myself, suspecting that whatever I said would only make things worse. So I remained silent.

"I don't blame you for not speaking," Opal said. "If it were me, I'd be too ashamed to say anything too."

"It isn't that," I said, finally finding my voice. "I just feel as if you've already made up your minds about me and that what I say won't change a thing."

"So what's this business about you calling the Virgin Mary a floozy?" the superintendent asked.

"I did no such thing. One of our newer attenders simply mentioned in Sunday school that he doubted the Virgin Birth and when Bea asked me about it, I admitted that I wasn't sure what to think of it myself. That's all I said. The next thing I know, it's being blown out of proportion, rumors are flying around, and I'm in hot water."

"Well, then, this is easily solved," the superintendent said. "Just stand in the pulpit and say you believe it, and we can put this whole thing behind us and move on. That'd satisfy everyone, wouldn't it?"

Opal nodded her head. "And I think he needs to publicly apologize for causing all this trouble in the first place."

"It's the least he should do," Fern said.

"I'm sure Sam is willing to apologize," the superintendent said. "Aren't you, Sam?"

"I never mind apologizing if I've done something wrong. But I've done nothing wrong."

"Well, Sam, that isn't quite true," the superintendent said. "You've questioned a bedrock principle of the church."

"Don't I have the freedom to do that? We're Quakers, after all. We don't have creeds. Aren't I allowed to express doubts or ask questions?"

"Not if it causes trouble," Fern said.

"Why does it need to cause trouble?" I asked. "Why can't questions be asked and people reflect on them without getting bent out of shape?"

"Now there's your problem, right there," Dale said. "We ought not question the Lord. If the Lord said His mother was a virgin, then that's good enough for me."

"Except the Lord never said it," I pointed out. "The Church said it about him. But the Church can be wrong. We've been wrong before."

"This is all very interesting," the superintendent said. "But I've got a two-hour drive ahead of me and need to get back home. So, Sam, if you could just apologize to these good people for stirring up trouble, we'll put this all behind us."

I sat quietly for a moment, thinking about what kind of minister I wanted to be, what kind of man I wanted to be.

"I won't do it," I said quietly. "I've done nothing wrong, and to apologize would be insincere."

"Well, Sam, I have no choice but to dismiss you."

Our superintendent had a bad habit of confusing himself with a bishop.

"You can't do that," I pointed out. "You don't have the authority. Only my congregation can dismiss me."

"Well, then, I suppose you'll just have to quit."

"I won't do any such thing."

"It's clear these people don't want you as their pastor."

"They represent a vocal minority who wouldn't be happy if Jesus were their pastor." I said it without thinking, felt bad for an instant, then got over it. "Besides, there are many others in the congregation who value my ministry and tell me so regularly."

"Well, your supposed supporters aren't here," Fern said. "If they even exist. And we're the elders. What do the rest of you think?"

"Nothin' personal, Sam," Dale said. "But I think it's time you went. We need new blood." He paused. "You know, Sam, sometimes I wonder if the Lord even called you to ministry. You don't seem to have a servant's heart."

"Did you think that last month when I was cooking your breakfast, washing your underwear, and trying to talk your wife into coming home?"

"What's that got to do with anything?" Dale asked, genuinely perplexed.

"You know what I think?" Opal said. "He's been nothin' but trouble. He doesn't even like organ music. Don't think I haven't noticed you squirm while Bea's playing. Next thing you know, he'll have drums and guitars in here and we'll be singing rock and roll."

H

"I'm inclined to agree with them," Fern said. "Your presence here is divisive. I think it's time you left. Do the rest of you approve?"

"Approve," they grumbled.

The superintendent glanced at his watch. "Sorry it turned out this way, Sam. Come see me sometime next week, and we'll see if maybe there's another church that'll have you. Though I think maybe you oughta lose that chip on your shoulder so you don't run into this sort of trouble again."

"I won't be coming by," I said. "I'm still the pastor of this church. This committee doesn't have the authority to fire me. They must have the approval of the meeting, which they've not done."

"There you go, quibbling over minor details again," Fern said. "That's just what we're talking about, Sam. You're always wanting to argue about things."

"Excuse me, Fern, but this is my livelihood we're talking about here. My children have become accustomed to eating."

I was starting to get irritated.

"We're not the only ones who don't like you," Opal said. "Stanley Farlow and his wife are thinking of leaving the church, and Bea's decided not to play the organ anymore."

There is a God in heaven, I thought to myself.

"If we can't fire you, then maybe you should just quit," Dale suggested.

"Sometimes that sounds very appealing," I admitted.

"It's settled then," Fern said. "Sam has quit. This meeting is adjourned."

The superintendent rose to his feet and clapped me on the back. "Takes a big man to admit that he's been wrong and to step aside for new leadership." He turned to Fern. "I'll have some new candidates for you to start interviewing next week. Did I mention my nephew's been looking for a pulpit?"

They walked up the stairs, discussing the nephew's sterling character, while I remained seated, trying to figure out what had just happened. I was beginning to suspect a trap had been set, and I'd blundered into it. For people with a history of integrity, Quakers sure could be sneaky. It occurred to me I should have feigned illness and stayed home.

I wasn't sure whether I was employed or not, but I knew when Fern got home, she'd start working the phone telling people I'd resigned, so I thought I'd beat her to the punch. I walked upstairs to my office and called Miriam Hodge, who answered the phone out of breath. "We just got home, Sam. How'd the meeting go?"

"I think I might have quit, but I'm not sure."

"What do you mean you're not sure?"

"It all happened so quick. One moment I was the pastor, and the next minute they were talking about hiring the superintendent's nephew."

"Him? He's a twerp. He's been fired from every church he's ever pastored."

"According to the superintendent, he's the greatest preacher since the Apostle Paul."

"Sam, you go on home and don't worry about this. I'll get it taken care of."

"Thank you, Miriam. Sorry to put you through this."

"It's not your fault, Sam. Don't give it a thought."

"Take care, Miriam."

"You too, Sam. Please know you're in my prayers."

"Thanks, Miriam. You're in mine."

I hung up the phone and walked home. A small part of me wanted to phone Miriam and tell her not to bother, that I'd go ahead and resign. I was tired of trying to keep people happy who took joy in being miserable. Tired of sacrificing my integrity on the altar of employment. The Quakers weren't the only game in town. Maybe the Episcopalians needed someone.

"How'd it go?" my wife asked, when I walked in the door.

"Either I was fired or I quit. I'm not sure. The upshot is that the superintendent wants his nephew to become the new pastor."

"That moron? What does he know about being a pastor?"

"That doesn't seem to be a concern. He apparently believes in the Virgin Birth, which seems to be all that matters these days."

She shook her head in disgust. "What's happened to Quakerism?"

"What do you mean?" I asked.

"I mean we used to be known as thoughtful people who respected the right of others to think and believe differently. What's happened to us?"

"I guess the fundamentalists have worn us down. I know I'm feeling worn down."

She glared at me, then stamped her foot, a sure sign I was about to be counseled. "Enough of that talk, Sam Gardner. You need to gird your loins and fight. They're nothing but bullies, the whole lot of them. Don't let them run you off. And for God's sake, don't let them hijack this beautiful religion."

"It's not that easy, honey. Quakers also believe in peace. I don't think it's appropriate for me to get caught up in a church fight."

"That doesn't seem to bother them," she said.

"That isn't the point. I can't choose how they behave, but I can choose how I'll behave. And I'm going to be kind."

"Then you're history," she predicted.

"So be it. At least I'll have my integrity."

She snorted. "Don't be getting all self-righteous on me, Sam. You have a responsibility to do what's best for the church. You're the pastor. You've been entrusted with leadership. Don't knuckle under."

"I'm too tired to think about that right now. I'm going to bed."

I don't know when she came to bed. I promptly fell asleep. I woke up the next morning, ate my breakfast, and puttered around the garage a few hours, studiously avoiding my wife and the subject of employment. I went to the office after lunch. As I pulled into the church parking lot, Dale was leaving, scrunched down in his car, looking sneaky. My office door was locked. My books were stacked on the floor of Frank's office.

"He changed the locks," Frank said. "He told me not to help you. Said you weren't the pastor anymore, that you'd quit."

"I did no such thing. How can I do my job if I don't have an office?"

"You could ask me for a key."

"He gave you a key?"

"Not exactly," Frank said. "I kind of slipped the extra one out of the package when he wasn't looking."

"That wasn't right, Frank."

"Don't be such a patsy, Sam. It's time you lived in the real world. Stick with me, kid, and I'll show you a few tricks."

For the first time in several days, I felt a rush of optimism, that I wasn't alone, that others would stand with me.

I reached down and picked up a stack of books. "If Dale or Fern call," I said, "tell them I'm working. In my office."

Twenty-three

The Petition

Two weeks had passed since I had unintentionally quit. It was now the first week of March, and Fern, Dale, and Opal were laboring to rally people to their cause, while Frank and Miriam were advising me to hold fast. I'd no sooner returned my books to their shelves, than Dale had snuck in the next night and removed them again. I put them back a second time, after which Frank changed the office lock, thwarting Dale's effort to oust me from my office.

Meanwhile, the troublesome trio made an elaborate show of placing plugs in their ears whenever I rose to preach. Bea Majors was off the organ, and Paul Iverson had taken her place with his guitar, which he'd learned to play in his hippie days. The downside was that he only knew hippie songs, so we tended to sing the same songs each Sunday—Bob Dylan and Woody Guthrie songs, with an occasional Peter, Paul, and Mary tune thrown in for good measure. Easter was a scant month away and I was encouraging him to expand his repertoire.

The superintendent's nephew had shown up the previous Sunday despite Frank's best efforts. He'd phoned the week before, asking

directions to Harmony. There are a handful of towns named Harmony in the United States and Frank had sent him to one two states
away.

He's not the sharpest knife in the drawer," Frank said. "He
showed up at a church, preached, then sat in the office for two days
before realizing they were Methodists."

Now he was at our church, circling like a vulture, ready to pick my
carcass clean. He was staying with Dale, sleeping on their fold-out
sofa. He'd been stopping by the meetinghouse each morning to see if
I'd vacated the office. I was practically living at the place to keep him
at bay.

"My uncle told me I'm the pastor," he complained each morning.
"You need to leave."

"Your uncle's not in charge," I pointed out. "He just thinks he is."

And so went our verbal sparring, back and forth each morning. I
would meet his thrusts with a parry, then send him on his way.

Dale went to the bank and tried to close the church accounts so I
couldn't be paid, but Vernley Stout, the bank president, told him it
required two signatures, neither of which was his. Even when Dale
stood in the lobby and prayed aloud for a cloud of locusts to descend
upon the Harmony Savings and Loan, Vernley was unruffled and
suggested Dale go annoy someone else. Dale retaliated by closing out
their anniversary cruise account, confident this would spell the bank's
ruination, though it appeared to absorb the three-dollar loss quite
nicely and go forward without a hitch.

Discouraged by my continued refusal to make their lives easier
and die, Dale, Fern, and Opal formed a secret committee to oust me.

But the secret was so well kept no one learned of the committee except for them, which hampered its effectiveness. I would never have learned about it, but they held it in the church basement one evening and Frank caught them.

"What have we here?" Frank asked. "A man and two women alone in the church with the lights turned low. I'm not one to think the worst of people, but this doesn't look too good. I hope no one asks me what I saw. I'd hate for this to get out."

That kept them quiet a few days.

This couldn't happen at a worse time. We are well into Lent, and though Quakers don't go for Lent in a big way, we have assumed some of its attendant burdens, like the annual Easter play the youth and children of the meeting present. Miriam Hodge was going to direct it, but then told me she couldn't save my job and direct the play at the same time, that she didn't have time to do both, so the play fell to me. I promptly handed it off to my wife, after promising to take her away for a long weekend after Easter.

It is the same play the youth perform every year, written by the late Juanita Harmon in 1959 as a tribute to her mother, whose crowning achievement was winning second place at the state fair four years in a row with her marigolds. The play is less about Easter and more about the beauty of God's creation. It would help if Jesus were mentioned in the play, but Juanita Harmon was an early New Ager and preferred to see God in flowers and trees and butterflies. When I was growing up, I always played the part of the daffodil. Of all the plays I was forced to perform in as a child, I liked that one the most, as none of the flowers had speaking parts. We simply had to smile and look radiant.

Dale has been opposed to the play since it first debuted. Each year he suggests one of the flowers give an altar call, but time confers a certain sacredness, even to church plays, and we've kept it unchanged.

I would take their effort to fire me more personally if it were something new, but Dale, Fern, and Opal have conspired to get rid of every pastor since 1962, when Dale first arrived on our shores. There is, I'm beginning to learn, a certain aspect of fundamentalism that requires the fires of division to be regularly stoked. Fundamentalists must be against something, usually a person who typifies everything they resent. There must always be an enemy, a convenient target upon which the wrath of God must fall. This year, the bull's-eye is pinned to my chest.

Pastor Taylor, my predecessor, survived by smiling a lot and agreeing with everyone. Though I remember he ate Tums by the truckload. An ever-present chalky smear ringed his mouth. If he had any doubts about the Virgin Birth, he never said so. In fact, he studiously avoided theology, which isn't easy when you're a minister, though he succeeded. Instead, he would talk about ten steps to a healthy marriage or six signs of a growing church. But he would readily concede there might be more steps or signs he hadn't considered. What ultimately prevented his termination was that he had the good sense to die before Dale could get him fired.

On the third Sunday in March, three weeks before Easter, I asked Dale, Fern, and Opal to meet with me after worship. By the close of worship, they were fit to be tied. Despite my encouragement to expand his play list, Paul Iverson had played Led Zeppelin's "Stairway to Heaven" for the third Sunday in a row.

I thanked him for playing a song with the word *heaven* in it, but suggested he might occasionally play a Fanny Crosby song, maybe "Pass Me Not, O Gentle Savior" or "Near the Cross."

"Fanny Crosby . . . Fanny Crosby . . . ," Paul mused aloud. "Didn't she sing backup for Joan Baez?"

"How about 'Kumbaya'? Do you know 'Kumbaya'?" I asked, pausing a moment to chew on a Tums.

"That was the Rolling Stones, right?"

I helped myself to another Tums.

My meeting with Dale, Fern, and Opal wasn't much better. They presented me with a list of thirty-five people whom the Lord had spoken to, saying it was time I left.

"Who's Althea Searcy?" I asked, scanning the list.

"That's my son Raymond's mother-in-law."

"But she doesn't even attend this church. Isn't she a Baptist?"

"What have you got against Baptists?"

"Nothing. I have friends who are Baptists. But this doesn't concern them."

"That's a fine how-do-you-do," Fern said. "You're all the time telling us to reach out to our Christian brothers and sisters and the first time we do, you slap us down."

"How long are we gonna have to listen to that rock music during church?" Opal asked.

"He's doing his best, Opal. Besides, now that Bea's not playing the organ, he's all we have."

She turned to the others. "I knew he'd end up blaming Bea for all of this."

I continued to scan the list of my detractors. "Albert Finchum's name is on here."

"You bet."

"But he's been dead six months."

"Well, it's a good thing, because your theology probably would have killed him," Fern said.

"I don't think Albert cared one way or the other about theology," I said.

Opal shook her head in disgust. "Now he's attacking the dead."

"What's Edith Barker's name doing on here?" I asked.

"She wants to see you go," Dale said.

"But she has Alzheimer's," I protested. "She doesn't know what she wants."

"Now he's attacking the sick and shut-ins," Opal moaned.

"Who in the world is Paul Davis?" I asked, returning to the list.

"He's my cousin from Alabama," Dale said. "I've told him all about you and he thinks you oughta leave too."

Frank stuck his head in the door. "Sorry for interrupting, Sam, but Uly Grant's grandma has been taken to the hospital in Cartersburg, and they want to know if you could hurry over there."

He turned to face the trio. "Don't you all have something better to do than keep Sam from his ministry?"

After they'd shuffled from the room, I turned to Frank. "Uly's grandparents have been dead ten years. What's going on?"

"Nothing. I just thought you wanted to be rid of them."

"Remind me to work on that raise for you."

"Jessie Peacock's here, and she'd like to talk."

I glanced at my watch. My Sunday dinner was getting cold. A pastor's lot in life—congealed gravy over cold mashed potatoes. "Okay, have her come in."

"Sorry to bother you, Sam," Jessie said, settling in the chair across from my desk. "But I've been hearing things about you and thought I ought to ask you myself."

"Sure, Jessie. What's on your mind?"

"Fern has been telling people you aren't a Christian."

"Yes, I'm aware of that."

"Do you know why she's saying that?"

"She thinks I don't believe in the Virgin Birth of Jesus," I explained.

"Do you?"

"I'll tell you what I told her. I don't know what to make of it."

Jessie sat quietly, thinking. "I'm not sure what to make of it either."

"I do know one thing," I said.

"What's that, Sam?"

"It's easier to believe things about Jesus than it is to do what he said. Maybe that's why Fern, Dale, and Opal talk so much about him, but don't seem all that eager to follow his teachings."

Jessie chuckled. "That would explain it, wouldn't it. So what do you think's gonna happen, Sam?"

"I think they're going to keep trying to get me fired," I speculated. "Did you hear about the petition they're asking people to sign?"

"Yes, Fern brought it by the house the other day and asked us to sign it. That's when she told us you weren't Christian. Asa told her she wouldn't know a Christian from a Cadillac."

I laughed. "How'd she take that?"

"Oh, she got all mad. Told him he wasn't a Christian either, then stormed out. Typical Fern."

Jessie rose to leave.

"Thanks for stopping by, Jessie."

"You hang in there, Sam. There are many of us here who appreciate your ministry."

"Thank you, friend."

She stopped halfway to the door. "By the way, who's that young man who's been coming to meeting the last couple of weeks? He's sitting with Dale and Dolores."

"That's the superintendent's nephew. He's been trying to get me fired. He wants to be the new minister here."

"Well, we'll just see about that," Jessie said, rather ominously.

The rest of the day was fairly quiet. I spent the next day with my mother, sorting through the last of my grandparents' possessions. It had taken only twelve years to cast off their belongings, which might be a record in this town of pack rats and savers.

I returned to the office on Tuesday and found Frank waiting for me. "I was just getting ready to call you. Did you hear what happened?"

"No."

"The superintendent's nephew is gone. Seems Dale found a bunch of empty beer cans in his car and sent him packing."

"Well, I'll be. Isn't that interesting?"

Frank chuckled. "Yeah, the funny thing is, I was over at Cartersburg yesterday and I saw Jessie Peacock coming out of the liquor store carrying a six-pack of Budweiser. I didn't know Jessie drank beer."

"She doesn't."

"Well, then, it must have been my imagination," Frank said.

"Sounds like it," I agreed.

"Then I probably shouldn't mention it to anyone."

"Probably not."

Dale stopped by a few hours later, demanding to see me. Frank ushered him into my office, but left the door open so he could eavesdrop.

"Hi, Dale. What brings you by here?"

"Matthew, chapter five, verses twenty-three and twenty-four."

I strained to remember that particular passage.

"Therefore if thou bring thy gift to the altar, and there rememberest that thy brother hath ought against thee; Leave there thy gift before the altar, and go thy way; first be reconciled to thy brother, and then come and offer thy gift."

"Oh, yes," I said. "Of course."

"Well?"

"Well what?" I asked.

"Is there somethin' you wanna say?" Dale prodded.

"Um, not that I know of. Did you have something specific in mind, Dale?"

"I just thought maybe you wanted to ask my forgiveness for the way you treated me."

"The way I treated you! I've not done anything to you, except cook your breakfast, wash your underwear, and save your marriage."

"But you're supposed to do those things. It's your job."

"No, Dale, it isn't. It's my job to equip the members of this church for the work of ministry. And I would love to do that, except I have to spend my time doing a bunch of other crap just to keep certain people in this church happy so I won't get fired."

"Ministers shouldn't cuss," Dale said.

"Church members shouldn't make their pastors so mad they lose their temper."

He began to say something, then thought better of it. He studied the carpet, tracing a design with the toe of his shoe. "Things are better between me and the missus."

"That's good, Dale. I'm glad to hear that."

"I guess maybe I oughta thank you for your help."

"That would be nice."

"Uh, well, thanks, Sam."

"You're welcome, Dale."

His stomach rumbled. "Wanna go to lunch?" he asked.

"Are you buying?"

He reached in his pocket for his wallet, opened it, then frowned. "As long as you don't order dessert."

"It's a deal, then."

"And if you want, you can stick around a little longer."

"Thank you, Dale. But what about the superintendent's nephew?"

"Sam, would you believe it if I told you there are some folks who claim to be Christian who don't act like Christians at all?"

"Really?"

"Yes," he said. "It's true." He appeared to regret having to shatter my illusions.

"And the superintendent's nephew was one of them?"

"You could say that," Dale said solemnly.

"I would never have guessed it."

Dale leaned toward me. "Drank like a fish," he whispered.

"What a shame."

"And you can bet his uncle's gonna hear about it," Dale assured me.

"Perhaps you shouldn't mention it. After all, he is young and just starting out. Why don't we pray for him instead."

"I thought about mailin' him a salvation sucker."

"That's very kind, Dale. I'm sure he'd appreciate that."

Lunch at the Coffee Cup was a hamburger and onion rings, dripping with grease, just the way I liked them. I didn't even feel guilty. It had been a hard month, and I'd earned it.

Twenty-four

Life Goes On

The annual Palm Sunday pageant, sponsored by the Harmony Ministerial Association, was actually held the Saturday before. It had been our church's turn to supply a Jesus. After the Fourth of July calamity, my son Levi refused such a visible public role, so Billy Grant was promoted from one of the multitudes rejoicing and praising God to the Messiah himself, which appeared to do wonders for his self-esteem.

It is a coveted role in our town, one that has launched many an illustrious career. Frank Gladden, the 1965 Jesus, went on to become the Midwest sales leader of Knapp Shoes, earning him and his wife an all-expense-paid trip to Pittsburgh and a crystal replica of the famous Knapp work shoe, complete with a steel toe for safety. It sits in his front window, illuminated by a spotlight, and is just one of the many tourist attractions our town has to offer.

The 1974 Jesus, Margaret Flynn, who was appointed to that lofty post in order to quell a feminine uprising in our town, now teaches at a liberal college in California where the students worship redwood trees and wouldn't know the Triune God if He kicked them in the shins, according to her sister, Dorothy, who put Margaret's name on the prayer list at the Baptist church in 1985, where it's remained ever since.

Billy Grant did an admirable job, managing to look both lordly and kindly at the same time. His ferret rode with him, peeking out from underneath his robe, sniffing the air and surveying the crowd, which grows smaller every year.

The Palm Sunday pageant used to be one of our town's larger events. The faithful would watch from the sidewalk, then troop off to Kivett's Five and Dime to buy their Easter baskets, green grass, and jelly beans. Then the fathers would take their sons to Morrison's Menswear to buy their Easter suits, while the women walked two doors down to Mrs. Mingle's dress shop for their Easter finery.

Now Morrison's and Mingle's are closed and the Christians drive over to the Wal-Mart in Cartersburg and eat at the Burger King. Boys don't wear suits anymore. The old people still dress up and seem dismayed that the younger people take Palm Sunday and Easter so casually.

The day before Palm Sunday, Harvey Muldock's daughter Susan drove out from the city with her husband, Bruce, and their four children to stay the weekend. They spend Palm Sunday with Harvey and Eunice, and have Easter at Bruce's parents in Amo, the next town over.

Their oldest child is sixteen. He's been hanging out with an anarchist group. He believes organized religion is a plot by the ruling class to keep the masses complacent. His mother made him dress up and go to church with them anyway. When he arrived at the meeting-house, he went to the rest room, took off his dress shirt, put on a black T-shirt, and then walked down front to the second row, where his parents were seated. Though I couldn't read his T-shirt from my chair behind the pulpit, I knew it had to be scandalous. Wives were elbowing their dozing husbands while parents covered their children's eyes. There were audible gasps as he walked toward the front.

When he entered the pew to sit, he turned and I caught a glimpse of his shirt. The words *If a Man Has a Good Car, He Doesn't Need to Be Saved* were printed on the back in crisp white letters. Fern was seated two rows behind him, glaring. Opal Majors wore a dazed expression. Dolores Hinshaw had placed her arm around Dale's shoulder and appeared to be restraining him.

I knew before the day was over I would be blamed for not having the ushers strip-search the teenagers to prevent such calamities, but even that prospect could not dull my joy. I've always loved Palm Sunday. Not even a budding anarchist could spoil it. Besides, I believe young people should rebel. It is the natural order of things, God's way of making their eventual departure from home less painful. Otherwise, we would be brokenhearted. This way, we're relieved to see them go.

"Nice shirt," I told him after church. "If I gave you the money, could you get one for me?" He sagged with disappointment. No young anarchist worth his salt wants the approval of the oppressive ruling class. I do the same thing whenever my son Levi listens to rap music. "Great song, son. Could you turn it up so I can sing along?"

That pretty well ruins it for him.

After church, we went to my parents' house for Sunday dinner. We tried to get out of it, but my mother was insistent. For years, she's served ham loaf for Sunday dinner, thinking my father liked it. He'd made the mistake of complimenting it, early in their marriage, in an effort to appease her after a marital spat. She's been making it ever since.

She served me two great slabs, which I managed to choke down with copious amounts of iced tea. I dropped my fork, which sent her scurrying back to the kitchen for a replacement. I used the opportunity to slip their dog a large chunk of ham loaf. He gobbled it down before realizing what it was, then scratched at the back door to be let out so he could eat grass and vomit the noxious lump of ham loaf back up.

I took off the next day, then spent much of the next week writing my Easter sermon, visiting the shut-ins, and arguing with my son Levi about being in the Easter play at church. He is a tall child and the only costume that fit him was the hollyhock.

"It's pink. I don't want to be a pink flower. The other kids will make fun of me."

"At least you're one of the bigger flowers," I pointed out. "When I was your age, they made me be the daffodil. The roses beat me up every year."

"How come we have to do this stupid play anyway?"

"Because we've always done it."

That wasn't the real reason. The real reason was that if we stopped doing this play, Dale would write a new one, probably something involving a live crucifixion.

The week flew by. The community Good Friday service was held at the Catholic church, which only served Communion to its own kind, while we Protestants looked on feeling like second cousins in the household of faith. When I was a child, Father Keffler was the priest and offered Communion to anyone who came forward. I thought at first it was because he was broad-minded, though I later learned he was far-sighted and wouldn't have recognized his own mother from two feet away. Now they have a new priest with 20/20 vision, so our town's ecumenism has been nipped in the bud.

I spent Saturday morning working with the Friendly Women, readying the meetinghouse for Easter. I found myself alone with Fern, helping arrange the memorial lilies around the platform. The other women were downstairs, baking cookies and cleaning the kitchen.

"I hate Easter," she said, placing a lily next to the pulpit.

I sensed she wasn't waiting for a response, so I remained silent.

She picked up another lily and placed it on the organ.

"Every year, it's the same thing," she said, her back turned to me. "A lily for my father, one for my mother, one for my sister, and me sitting in the pew all by myself with all my family gone. Just me, staring at all these stupid lilies."

"Not all your family's gone," I said. "You still have your church family."

"It's not the same."

I suspected she was right, so I didn't disagree.

"My ankles are killing me. I have to sit down."

I looked at her ankles. They were swelling out over the tops of her shoes, like sausages crammed in too small a casing.

"Don't ever get old, Sam. Everyone you love is dead, and your ankles hurt."

"Thanks for the tip, Fern. I'll try not to age."

The corners of her mouth twitched in something resembling a smile.

It's funny how the curtain parts and you glimpse a dimension of someone you didn't know existed. I occasionally dream of extra rooms in my home, rooms I didn't know existed. I hadn't understood the dream until now.

I've known Fern since 1966, when she was my first-grade teacher. It was an inauspicious start to my education. By the second week, I'd concluded Fern was a grouch and never bothered to change my opinion. But sitting in the meetinghouse with her, I realized there were other dimensions to her life I'd overlooked, other rooms I hadn't noticed—her loneliness, her sorrow, her disappointment with life.

I sat beside her on the first pew. "I know having a church family isn't the same as having your parents and sister back. But you are important to us, Fern. I know you and I have had our disagreements, but it doesn't mean I don't care about you."

Her chin trembled. A tear leaked from her left eye and caught in the folds of her cheek.

"Even after I tried to get you fired?"

"Yes, Fern, even after that."

She sniffed. I handed her my handkerchief. "I don't know why I do things like that."

"We all do things we later regret. We're human. We make mistakes." I paused. "What are you doing for Easter, Fern?"

"I thought I'd drive down to the interstate and get a fish sandwich at the McDonald's."

"By yourself?"

"I've done it before. It's okay."

"We're having Easter dinner at my parents' house. Why don't you come eat with us? I'm sure Mom and Dad would love to have you."

"You mean it?"

"I certainly do, Fern."

"After all I've done to you?"

"Fern, that was yesterday. Today's another day. Let's move on."

She leaned over into me. "Thank you, Sam."

We sat there for some time, Fern and I, not saying anything. Fern smelled like my grandmother. I closed my eyes. My mind rewound to my childhood. I was sitting with my grandmother on their swing underneath their maple tree, while my grandfather mowed the yard. I could hear the snickety-clip of the lawn mower and see the clipped remnants of grass swarming softly like gnats around the mower.

But life goes on.

I lifted my arm around Fern and squeezed her to me. "We'll eat tomorrow around two, but you can come early if you want."

"Thank you, Sam."

I rose to my feet and walked out, glancing back when I reached the doorway. Fern was still seated, looking at the lilies, dabbing at her eyes with my handkerchief, dwelling in rooms I'd never known existed.

In addition to writing, Philip Gulley also enjoys the ministry of speaking. If you would like more information, please contact:

David Leonards
3612 North Washington Boulevard
Indianapolis, IN 46205-3592
317-926-7566
ieb@prodigy.net

If you would like to correspond directly with Philip Gulley, please send mail to:

Philip Gulley
c/o HarperSanFrancisco
353 Sacramento St.
Suite 500
San Francisco, CA 94111

Register for your free subscription to the Harmony e-newspaper

Harmony Herald

Go to www.harmonyherald.com

ALSO BY PHILIP GULLEY